Sarah's Playmates
A Wild West Erotic Adventure

By Virginia Wade

This is a work of fiction. Names, characters, places, and incidents either are the product of the author's imagination or are used fictitiously, and any resemblance to any persons, living or dead, business establishments, events, or locales is entirely coincidental.

Sarah's Playmates, A Wild West Erotic Adventure

All rights reserved.

Published by I Love Stacy
Copyright © 2012 by Virginia Wade
Cover art by Adelaide Cooper
ISBN: 1480070432
ISBN-13: 978-1480070431

Email: virginia@virginia-wade-erotica.com

This book is protected under the copyright laws of the United States of America. Any reproductions or other unauthorized use of the material or artwork herein is prohibited without the express written permission of the author.

First Edition: October 2012
Second Edition: March 2013

Also available in paperback by Virginia Wade

Cum For Bigfoot, Volume One
Cum For Bigfoot, Volume Two
Jane's Playmates: A Tarzan and Jane Erotic Adventure
Sarah's Playmates: A Wild West Erotic Adventure
Siren Island: An erotic adventure
The Filthy Classics Collection
Lily

Coming soon to paperback

Cum For The Viking
The Stacy Series, Volume One
The Stacy Series, Volume Two

Chapter One

I stood on the railway platform, staring out at the gathering throng waiting to board the train. My traveling companion, Millie Doyle, waved a fan over her face, her ivory complexion marred with small red circles. The humidity at this time of year was oppressive, and the layers of clothing, the camisole, drawers, and corset were necessary, but challenging when it came to staying comfortable.

"We'll look like wilted cabbage before the day's out," said Millie in a lilting Irish accent. She pointed. "There's our man with the bags."

I pivoted in the other direction, seeing a person dressed in a striped vest and trousers, dragging a heavy looking trunk. Another man was behind him, clutching what I recognized as my own bag. "Good morning, Ladies." He tipped his hat. "You would be Sarah Collins, I presume?"

"Yes, I am."

He grinned pleasingly. "We're due to board any minute."

"Thank St. Patrick," muttered Millie. Wisps of strawberry blonde hair floated around her pretty face. She had been my mother's maid, and upon arriving in America, her position in the family had improved. I was privileged to have her as my companion, and she would accompany me to California.

A whistle blew and the doors opened. "All aboard!"

Excitement raced through me because my adventure was about to begin. I held the ticket in a gloved hand, my fingers trembling. My fiancé, Edmund Lakewood, waited for me in Chicago. The engagement ring I wore held a deep blue sapphire flanked by two large diamonds. Although it was hidden under my glove, I could feel the weight of its prominence. We had been engaged for more than a year, and, within two weeks, I would be his wife.

The porter took my hand, helping me ascend the steps. "Thank you."

I had been born in the jungles of Africa, where my mother had gone to find her father, the famous explorer Author Tennent. I'd spent my childhood in the wild and untamed beauty of the Congo. My mother, Jane Tennent Collins, was an adventurous spirit of unequaled loveliness. We had left Africa to live in England, because she wanted me to have an education and to know my family. Upon Author's death, we crossed the Atlantic, leaving behind the gray skies and rain to begin a new life in the sunny state of California.

The porter led us to a first class compartment with its own sleeping car. We would be traveling in luxury, the gleaming wood and plush seating affording all the comforts of home. Millie rushed to open a window; a sticky breeze filled the space along with the acrid smell of burning coal.

"Come sit with me," she said, removing her straw bonnet. "There's a breeze here."

I joined her on a plush, red velvet seat, as the men dragged the trunks in, placing them against a wall. "I'd wave goodbye, but there's no one to see me off."

"They'll greet you on the other side." Her smile revealed dimples.

"I can't wait to see Chicago!" I glanced out the window at the chaos. "Do you think we'll encounter Indians?"

"I hope not." She looked horrified. "They're proper

heathens, mind you. They'd best stay far away or I'll beat them with my shillelagh." I laughed at that mental image, and the porters stared at me. "Off with you now." She waved at them. "You've done your job." They tipped their hats and left hastily. "And don't be expecting a tip either."

I had spent years with various African tribes, including the nefarious *Azande*, who filed their teeth to sharp points and practiced cannibalism. What could possibly be worse than that? "I'm starving."

"Let's freshen up and find the dining car."

"That's a capital idea, Millie."

An hour later, we sat facing each other in a lengthy car graced with oversized windows. Green fields stretched as far as the eye could see, punctuated by the occasional farm. The top portions of the windows were open, creating a delightful breeze. Sipping my tea, I stared happily at the scenery, knowing that with each passing mile, we drew nearer to Chicago, where my fiancé was waiting to accompany me to California.

A porter approached. "You have a telegram, Ms. Collins."

I took the small piece of paper. "Thank you."

"Must I ask from whom?"

I smiled. "No, you mustn't. You know, Millie." The message was from Edmund.

DARLING SARAH STOP MY ANTICIPATION OF YOUR ARRIVAL GROWS BY THE HOUR STOP MAY YOU HAVE A SAFE AND FELICITOUS JOURNEY STOP YOU ARE ALWAYS IN MY THOUGHTS AND PRAYERS STOP- EDMUND.

"He's besotted with you, and why wouldn't he be?"

Edmund hailed from a wealthy family; his father

3

was a prominent Senator. I had met him in New York, while vising my parents before they decided to relocate west. I had delayed the trip because I had hoped that he would ask for my hand in marriage, and he had! It was my proudest achievement to date, despite earning a diploma from Girton College. I relished the idea of maintaining my own home and having children. Millie was kind enough to offer me "special" instruction on the intimacies between men and women, which she was versed in. Her husband had died of tuberculosis three years after they had been married. Thinking about our nightly lessons, the tiniest hint of a blush mantled my cheeks.

"What shall we eat for supper?" Millie held a menu. "The Macaronied Beef sounds good." The child across from us had his napkin tucked into his shirt. He swung his legs happily, until his mother made him stop. "Sarah?"

"Hm?"

"Aren't you hungry?"

I glanced at the menu. "Of course."

That evening, as the train rocked and swayed, I dressed for bed in a white cotton nightgown with a high neckline. I sat in a chair and held a novel, while Millie used the facilities. She returned a few minutes later.

"What are you reading?"

"One of your books by Lady Morgan."

"Which one?"

"*The Wild Irish Girl.*"

"Oh, for heaven's sakes. Put it away."

"But it's good." She hated it when I went through her things.

"Your time would be better spent learning all the little ways you can please your husband."

I inhaled a long, shuddering breath. "Is a lesson in my future?"

"It is indeed."

"Is the door locked?"

"Of course."

"What's on the agenda tonight?"

She turned down the lamp. "Something slightly unorthodox, but highly stimulating. I'll perform it on you, and then you'll know how to do it for Edmund."

"How will I know if he'll like it?" She had removed her basque, dropping the fitted bodice on a chair. Her fingers deftly worked the tiny buttons on the shirt.

I slid from the bed. "I'll help." I began to untie her corset.

"Oh, don't bother with the laces. I'll unfasten it at the front." She seemed slightly impatient tonight.

"Then my work is done."

I snatched a wine glass off a table and had a sip, eyeing her. She had removed her skirt and bustle, which were now draped over the back of a chair. Petticoats were next, then her camisole and drawers. At last, her pale, creamy skin was revealed. I shivered, remembering the first time she had approached me with the idea for "special instructions". This was all in the vein of learning how to please my husband, of course. How knowing a woman intimately would accomplish this feat was beyond me, and, perhaps, it didn't matter. That first lesson had produced such extraordinary pleasure, I was more than willing to continue and learn for as long as Millie deemed it necessary.

She released her hair, the lustrous strawberry locks falling down her back. Her breasts were wonderfully full and contoured, with rosy tips that hardened to stiff peaks. Knowing that the evening would end with us entwined, moaning, and perspiring left me suddenly weak. I held the table, as the train rocked, the repetitive sound of the running gear moving over the tracks.

She sat on the bed, holding out her hand. "Come here."

I left the glass on the table and approached, while little crickets jumped in my tummy. "What's the lesson tonight?"

"Something wonderful."

I shivered at the husky tone in her voice. "It's always wonderful."

"Take your nightgown off." The garment went over my head and landed at my feet. Her breath hissed through her teeth. "You're always so lovely, Sarah. Your body is sheer perfection." She touched my breasts, which were nearly as large as hers. "These are sinful, my dear. You've been blessed with such beauty."

"So have you." I stroked the side of her face, feeling the softness of her skin. "I don't know why you haven't remarried. I see the way men look at you."

"Come sit." She patted the bed. "My husband, as the saying goes, was always in the field when the luck was on the road." She touched my hair. "He was sick when I married him, but I didn't know how bad it was. Then there was the drinking."

"I'm sorry, Millie."

She sighed. "He preferred whiskey to sex anyway. Oh, it doesn't matter. It was long ago."

"I can't wait to be married."

"Men are wondrous creatures, but…they're not Gods. They aren't perfect. They drink and they fight and they…" She shrugged.

"What?"

"They have all the power. When you're married,

6

you'll not be able to do as you please." She noted my expression. "I won't lie to you, Sarah. It's not all wine and roses. You must choose carefully."

"You don't think Edmund is the right choice? But I'm fond of him."

"He's…a respectable man from a good family. You…you've made your parents proud."

I sensed her reservation. "But…?"

"Oh, my dear. He's a fine gentleman. I just wonder…"

"What?"

"Well, he's quite domineering. You've such a gentle spirit. I worry that he might crush it."

She'd never spoken like this before. "Really?" It occurred to me that I should be angry that she was finding fault with my betrothed. She wasn't a family member. She was essentially an employee. Her job was to be my chaperone.

"I've said too much." She looked contrite. "You're such a lovely young woman." Her attention was on my lips. "What a luscious mouth. I should kiss it."

A lightning bolt of tremors erupted in my tummy. "I need to practice, Millie. My husband deserves a wife who knows how to please him."

"Oh, yes," she breathed. "He does."

Chapter Two

Her lips met mine, igniting a burst of sensation that reverberated through my nerve endings like the scorched grass of a burning field. As her tongue slid into my mouth, my fingers gripped her shoulders, feeling the thinness of her frame. She held my face, deepening the kiss and leaning further into me.

"Attack me with your tongue, Sarah. Don't hold back." I drove in, sliding against her soft wetness. "Um…yes…that's it."

Her hands followed the line of my neck to my shoulders, where she gently massaged me. From there they roamed to my breasts, the weight of the globes filling her palms. A nipple was suddenly caught between her thumb and forefinger, gently compressed.

"Oh!" I gasped, feeling a rush of heat. "Oh, Millie." Her kisses descended to my throat, and I tilted my head back to allow her better access. "Will my husband do this?" I sounded breathless.

"Yes."

"I can't wait to be married."

"You can have your fun now, my dear. You needn't wait."

"Oh, yes, Millie. I won't tell a soul about this. It's…too good."

"No, Edmund mustn't know. These things women can do together, and they…are private. Lay down."

I fell to the thin mattress. "What now?"

Her gaze rested on my breasts. "Indulge me for a moment."

"Of course."

She rubbed her face against my breasts, which she had pressed together. Her touch was softness personified and feathery light, forcing my hips off the bed, my body instinctively wanting more. I hadn't meant to react this way, but I wasn't in control. A shocking dampness had developed between my legs, and, as she sucked a nipple into her mouth, a rather loud and unladylike moan escaped me.

"Millie!" Both nipples were toyed with and suckled; the tips were wet and hard. "What other plans do you have?" I needed so much more.

"Someone's impatient."

"No…I…well…maybe…" I smiled, staring at the inlay ceiling. The train continued on, the car shaking gently. "I…you should do what you did to me the other night." Just thinking about her tongue in my pussy brought a rosy flush to my face.

"I have something else in mind."

I swallowed my disappointment. "All right."

"You'll like it, Sarah," she chuckled. "Lay on your stomach." Something unidentifiable sparked in her green eyes.

"On my stomach?"

"Yes."

"Very well." I turned over, offering her by backside. "Now what?"

Her hand touched the indentation in my lower back. "You've such beautiful skin." Fingers grazed a rounded cheek. "Your bottom is…delicious looking. So round and firm."

Her words had me trembling with anticipation. "What will you do?"

"Some men enjoy it when women play with them."

"How do you mean?"

Her finger drifted to the crack of my ass. "They like to feel a tongue in here."

I gasped, "No!"

"I'll show you, and you can decide."

I turned to look at her. "But…that's perverse."

"Not at all."

"It's dirty. Oh, truly, Millie. It's filthy."

"It's sensual." She patted my back. "Now close your eyes and relax. Let me do all the work. All you have to do is feel."

"Oh, my goodness. You're not really serious about this?"

"Of course."

I groaned, partially out of embarrassment, but mostly because I throbbed, thinking about how naughty it would be. What she suggested was shocking, yet I was far too intrigued to stop her.

Her lips were on my cheek. "I love the way this curves. It's so round and beautiful." She massaged me, pressing my flesh together and apart, exposing my little hole. "I don't mind slightly smelly places. I'll clean you with my tongue."

"Millie!" I was profoundly stunned, but far too aroused to do anything about it. I couldn't believe that she was actually going to…lick that part of me. It was wonderful being touched here; the feel of her kneading my flesh was pleasurable. Hot breath lingered near my entrance, and I buried my face in a pillow, stiffening.

"Relax," she purred.

"But I must smell horrible. It's such a dirty place."

"No, my dear. I can't wait to taste you." Kisses fell while her fingers massaged my cheeks, hiding and exposing my hole. She shifted on the bed, separating my thighs.

"Oh!" She blew air against my crack, and I felt the effects lower, in my pussy, which I knew was dripping with the cream of my excitement. "Oh, my." Her nose rubbed my skin, and I cringed thinking of how smelly I must be.

Her tongue flicked out, wetting me. "Now, Sarah. Some men do like this."

"Did your husband?" My voice sounded muffled in the pillow.

"I'd never done it to him."

"Oh." Then how did she know men enjoyed this? Her tongue lapped against me, nearing the puckered edges. I closed my eyes, enjoying the sensation. She stroked that unmentionable place, and I gasped.

"There. That wasn't so bad, was it?"

"No."

"Of course not." She settled in, her body was between my legs, and her hands held my cheeks apart, exposing me entirely. "Now I'm going to eat you, Sarah. I'm going to fuck you with my tongue."

"Millie!" I'd never heard her talk like this before.

"Men like it when their prim and proper wives turn into whores in the bedroom."

"Oh, now that's ridiculous." I glanced over my shoulder.

"Lay down. We've had enough talking."

My forehead was on the pillow. "I won't like it."

"You will. Now shut up, and let me fuck you."

I wanted to reply, but as her tongue prodded me, leaving a swath of heated wetness, the words died in my mouth. The sensation was so deliciously wicked; I closed my eyes, reveling in the new and unique feeling. She held my cheeks apart, while she licked across the bumpy edges of my rectum. I didn't want to enjoy it, but I was helplessly drowning in the decadence of the treatment.

"You're opening nicely."

"Oh, Millie…this is dirty." She pressed her tongue in further, softening the tight bands of muscles. The more she did this, the better it felt.

"I'm curious."

I raised my head. "About what?"

"If you're aroused." Her finger brushed against my slit.

"Oh, my!"

"You're very wet."

She stroked an area so sensitive it began to throb and vibrate. I lifted my ass into the air. "Oh! OH!"

"I think you like that." I moaned in reply. "I know what I'll do now." Soft kisses fell to my heated flesh, as a finger began to slide into my wetness. I hid my face in the pillow, and, when she licked my anus, I shuddered with the onslaught of a thousand pleasurable spasms. "Do you want more?"

"Yes, Millie," I gasped. "Oh…yes."

"Good."

Her attention centered on my orifices, one hand rubbing my slit, thereby brushing my clit, while her tongue drove into the constricted bands of my hole. This had me panting, low and shallow, the air barely getting in deep enough to sustain me. I sounded as if I had been running, but I didn't want her to stop. A finger slid deep, my virgin pussy stretching to accommodate it. All the while, her tongue bathed my rectum, as copious amounts of saliva dribbled to the bedding.

"Oh, Milly. It's so good. Sooo…good." She said nothing, but in response, a second finger breached my honeyed walls. "Yes!" I thrust my ass up, driving her tongue in deeper. "More! Do it to me more!" The first time she had entered me, several weeks ago, it had hurt. Now there was nothing but mind-blowing pleasure, and I didn't want it to end. She began to rub something so sensitive; my panting sounded louder than the rumblings of the train. "I can't! I can't! Oh, God," I cried, my entire body trembling. "It's so good!" She said nothing, because her tongue was so far in my bottom, I could feel it wiggling back and forth, wrapping around the inner edges of my muscles. This, coupled with her fingers, sent me over the edge, like a boat in a whirlpool. "Millie! OH! MILLIE!" I shuddered, sputtering something incoherent, collapsing against the pillow, while she reamed my pussy, increasing the pleasure of each and every convulsion.

"I knew you'd like it."

"It was wicked good. Oh, Lord. I'll have to confess on Sunday."

"You're not Catholic," she laughed. "Leave the confessing to me. I'm the bigger sinner."

I turned to look at her. "You've corrupted me. No man could pleasure me like you do. That's the truth, isn't it?"

Her expression was vague. "They don't know the first thing about women, Sarah. I don't want to lie to you. They get drunk, they rut, and five minutes later, it's over."

"Is it really *that* bad?"

"My Shaun was like that."

I sat up and hugged her. "I'm sorry. Thank you for being honest. You've been keeping that a secret for a long time."

Her arms went around me. "I love the feel of a

woman, Sarah. I love the softness and the closeness. I've always been drawn to them." Her tone lowered to a husky drawl. "There's something I want you to do to me."

I glanced at her. "What's that?"

Her smile was mischievous.

Chapter Three

She lay against the pillow, spreading her legs. The thatch of strawberry blonde hair in her center had been trimmed. We both preferred to keep the unruly hair under some semblance of control. Getting rid of it altogether would be a dream, but only whores practiced that type of thing.

"What do you want me to do to you?"

Her fingers dipped into her snatch. "Come lick me. Make me wet."

"You're already wet."

"Make me drip."

I touched her leg. "You like it when I do that, don't you?"

"You know I do."

"Haven't you ever had a man who's satisfied you? Wasn't Shaun able? Not even once?"

"No, my dear. Men are clueless. The only true pleasure I've ever found was with a woman. Why do you think I haven't remarried? I'd rather have secret sex and have it satisfying, than a drunk brute who shits the bed."

"Millie!" I laughed. "That's far too descriptive."

"When you're married and your husband leaves you longing for more, send a letter, and I'll visit." She sat up and moved the hair out of my face. "I'll do all those naughty things you like, and you'll tremble under my tongue, screaming with pleasure."

"Oh, Millie. You really are a wicked woman."

"We have so few advantages, Sarah. I know you dream of marriage and a house and children, but none of that can make you feel as good as I can. When your husband finds a mistress and your bed is cold, I can warm you." She touched my tummy. "I'll light the fire inside of you, and you'll crave me."

"You're shameless. If my mother knew of your perversions, she'd never have let you chaperone me."

"I've heard a tale or two about your mother."

This had my attention. "What have you heard?"

"It's of no matter now, my dear. We can discuss it later." She took my hand. "Won't you touch me?"

"Of course."

She reclined on the bed. "I want your tongue here and your fingers in me here."

"That's quite specific." My grin was mildly sheepish.

"We shouldn't be afraid to express what we want."

"And we aren't."

"This is our private sanctuary. No one has to know what we do."

"And no one will," I giggled. "I do so enjoy being corrupted. I love what you did to me. It was so naughty."

"Maybe you can do it to me someday."

"I should."

She pointed to her pussy. "Come lick me, darling. I'm aching for you."

I settled between her thighs, inhaling a mildly musky odor. "You're already wet."

"You've done this to me."

"I'm going to do more to you than that."

"Yes," she breathed. "I want your tongue."

I kissed her thigh, feeling her heated skin. Tiny kisses led me to the shorn thatch of pubic hair and her little nub, which wasn't so little. My clitoris was small and hidden, but Millie's was the size of a marble, and it protruded when she was aroused. The lump thrust out, waiting for me to play with it.

"Oh, girl. Do it."

"Patience, Millie. Patience."

"I'm not a bloody doctor! I want you to fuck me."

"My goodness. I'm getting there." Her fierce Irish nature was in evidence. "I love your little nub. It's so big."

She threw her head against the pillow. "Suck on the damn thing, will you!"

I smacked her thigh. "You're being a brat. Now stop that."

"Ooohh…" she hissed through her teeth, "just suck me!" My tongue touched the tip of the protruding lump. "Yes, girl, yes! More of that. More!" She grabbed my hand. "Put your fingers in me. Start with two, and work your way up. Don't be shy. Don't stop until they're all in there."

I gasped, "Millie!" The violence of her passion was somewhat astounding.

"Just do it."

"Something's gotten into you."

"I want you in me!" My mouth closed around the little bead. "Oh, yes! Oh, God."

I settled in, scooting closer. Then I ran my tongue up her slit, tasting her saltiness. My thumbs separated her labia, exposing her dripping hole. The first time I had done this I had been less than eager to enter something that wet and musky. But, now, it didn't bother me at all, and, as I wiggled inside of her, I was rewarded with low and guttural moans. Leaving the sodden hole, I focused on the protruding clitoris, which was something fun to play with. The lump had grown even bigger, jutting from her flesh. I pushed against it with my tongue, eliciting another round of gasps and moans. Then, as I slid a finger inside of her, I closed around the object, massaging it with my tongue. I knew I had to be gentle, because it was highly sensitive, and, if I stimulated her too harshly, the pleasure would become pain…and we certainly couldn't have that.

"Oh-oh-oh! More fingers! More fingers!"

A second drove in easily, and I thought to give the third, but I was too busy compressing her clit between my lips. I played with the tiny cock, licking and prodding it, over and over.

"More fingers, girl!" she hissed. "Now!"

"As you wish."

A third joined the two, and I slid them in and out, massaging her passage, which gleamed with wetness. All the while, I focused on her nub, laving it persistently. Her tummy rose and fell with each breath. She'd closed her eyes, and her hands had curled into fists, which rested on her sides. It was exciting to know that I could affect a person in this way, that my touch and skill at lovemaking could make a woman pant and moan and scream with pleasure.

"More!"

A fourth finger drove in deep, opening her further. I rotated my wrist carefully, easing into something that felt hot and wet. Her muscles clamped around me, contracting and releasing. My tongue worked the engorged nub, leaving it dripping with saliva, which ran down her buttcrack to the bedding.

"Oh, yes…more…the whole hand. I want it all…please."

"Doesn't it hurt?" I was mildly alarmed.

"No, girl. Stop sucking, and focus on giving me everything I want." She manipulated her swollen clitoris. "Fuck me good. Don't hold back."

"Millie!"

"Your hands are small. It's marvelous. I adore the feeling."

The wetness of her orifice lubricated my hand, allowing it to slide in further. While she stroked herself, I drove deeper, burying my hand to the wrist. "It's in now."

"Yes," she hissed. "Keep doing that. It's lovely, my dear. Ooohh…sooooo…lovely…"

"This is dirty, Millie."

"Call me names. Call me a whore."

"I can't do that," I gasped.

"Fuck me harder, and call me a whore. Do it!" She worked her clit feverishly; the hardened object was fully engorged.

"You're a dirty whore, Millie. Is that what you want to hear?"

"Yes!"

"Your sexual needs are immoral."

"Oh, yes."

"You took my virginity."

"Oh, dear Lord, I did."

"Are you sorry for that?"

"No."

"You shameless slut. You dirty whore!"

"Oh, Sarah…" She moaned so loud, I thought the porter might hear. "I'm sooooo…oh, dear…God…have mercy."

I increased the pressure, rotating my hand and massaging her deeply. Her pussy clamped around me, the wetness reached above my wrist. "You're a whore, Millie! You filthy slut."

"Ooohhh…Sarah…oooohhhh…" She shuddered, her head lifting off the pillow, while her tummy quivered and her thighs shook. The muscles in her cunt contracted, gripping my hand like a vice. "Ooohhh…Lord…that was good. That was exactly what I needed."

My hand slid free. "We need to wash up."

"Oh, Sarah. That was marvelous. You'll have to do that to me again soon. I adore having a hand in me."

I felt quite smug at the moment. "I'm learning a good bit on this trip. It's been rather educational."

"You silly trollop!" She hugged me. "I'll miss you when you're married and settled."

"You'll have to visit," I grinned, "often."

The next day we sat in the dining car enjoying lunch. I ate salmon cutlets, while Millie devoured An Ambushed Trifle, which was more like a decadent dessert than a proper meal. The fellow diners talked and laughed, the women wearing pretty hats and the men in ascot ties and bowlers. We had left the station in Ohio ten minutes ago, and new passengers had joined us.

"You're lovely this morning, Sarah."

I sipped tea. "Thank you, Millie. So are you."

"You're one of the most beautiful women I've ever seen."

This declaration was a surprise. "My goodness."

"Your mother is beautiful, but you…you've surpassed her."

"It must be my Texas ancestry. Everyone says the Tennent bloodline is polluted." This thought brought a smile to my face. My mother had married a rough and tumble Texan, and society had been scandalized. I was daddy's girl and had always been. He was the most important man in my life, until the day I married.

"None of that matters. Your mother's a wealthy woman. Society forgave her. They're just jealous that she's sown her oats in greener pastures."

"It was a dream for her to come to America."

"That it was, my gir—"

There seemed to be a commotion in the next car. Something loud popped, which sounded like a firecracker. Heads turned around, alarmed. I glanced at Millie. "What's happening?"

A porter dashed into the car, his face was as white as parchment. "Robbers! We're being robbed! Hide your valuables!"

Chapter Four

Pandemonium erupted after this shocking announcement. Plates and glasses fell, smashing to the wooden floor, as passengers scurried to the other end of the car and through the connecting portion of the train to the next compartment. Millie was caught up in the rush, and we were separated.

"Millie!"

"Follow me, child! Sarah!"

I stumbled over my own feet, landing on my tummy. The constriction of the corset forced the air out of my lungs, and I struggled to breathe. My hat had fallen off, and several pins came loose, releasing a portion of perfectly coiffed hair. Struggling to sit, I turned and gasped. A revolver was aimed at my face.

"Put that down, Buck! You don't point a gun at a lady, you numbskull. Go on, and get the others." Paralyzed by fear, I could only stare at the man before me, who stood with his feet apart. The ruffian who held the gun dashed to the other car. "Well, ain't you pretty." He knelt before me. "What's your name, honey?"

"S-Sarah."

He wore scuffed boots, wrinkled trousers, and an ill-fitting jacket. His tawny hair needed trimming, and several days' worth of stubble graced a distractingly handsome countenance. His eyes blazed with interest. The irises were a warm chocolate color with flecks of gray.

"Are you injured?"

"No." My voice sounded tiny.

"Let me help you up." Before I could object, he

wrapped his hands around my arms and hauled me to my feet. I stood entirely too close to him.

"Oh!"

"This could go either of two ways, Miss. You can hand over your cash and jewelry without a fuss, or I can take it from your person. The choice is yours." My mouth formed a circle, but no words came out. He shook me. "Are we understandin' one another?"

"Ouf!" I smacked him in the face, surprising us both. "Don't touch me!"

He laughed; the timber in his voice was surprisingly pleasant. "That's the fighting spirit. I was startin' to worry you might be a simpleton." His grin produced small lines around his eyes. "This looks interesting." He held my gold locket.

"You can't have that. It's a family heirloom."

"Is that so?" He weighed the heavy pendant in his hand. "Looks expensive."

I pushed him. "Stop that!"

"This ain't no negotiation, darlin'. I'm here to rob you. Take it off."

Tears were in my eyes. "The only pictures of my parents I have are in there. You can't take my locket."

His gaze followed the single tear that slid down my cheek. He swallowed visibly. "What else you got?"

"I-I have my engagement ring."

"Let's see it."

I pulled off the glove and held up my hand. He whistled through his teeth. "That's some ring. You snagged yourself a rich one, eh?"

My ire rose. "My fiancé is a respectable man. He's educated and refined. His father's a United States senator. When I'm finished being robbed and manhandled, I'll be sure to send a telegram to Senator

Lakewood. He'll know exactly what's happened here today, sir."

"I like a woman with a sturdy backbone. There's a fire in your belly. I might just be jealous of that future husband of yours."

His response surprised me. I was at a loss.

"Gimme the ring."

I threw it at him. "Choke on it!" He struggled to catch the item, anger flaring in his eyes. Shoving the sapphire and diamond ring into a pocket, he advanced, grabbing me. "Now I want the locket."

"No!"

"You don't have a choice, darlin'. Hand it over."

"It's the only reminder I have of my grandmother." I closed my fist around the pendant. "It belongs to my family. It's for my daughter…when I have one. You can't have it, you horrible man."

His arm snaked around my back, drawing me against the firm expanse of his chest. He smelled of musk and perspiration with a hint of leather. "Now you listen closely, little lady. If you don't hand over that necklace, I'll…I'll be liable to do something you'll find repulsive."

"I'm already repulsed." This lie slid easily off my tongue. The proximity of our bodies was alarming, but what was even more so was the tingling that registered in my tummy.

His look smoldered. "Perhaps, a trade's in order."

"You have nothing I want. Unhand me, sir!" I pushed against him, feeling a wall of sinew and muscle.

"I'd be willin' to let the necklace go, if you give me a kiss."

I gasped. "You'll receive no such thing!"

"Savin' them kisses for your fiancé?"

An image of Millie, naked and panting filled my mind. "Y-you let me go!"

"Then give me the necklace."

"No!"

"So be it."

He grasped my face, holding me in place as his lips descended, covering my mouth. I tried to kick him, but layers of petticoats and bustles prevented me from affecting him in any possible way. I had never kissed a man before. Edmund had given me several chaste pecks on the cheek, but he wouldn't have dared take it any further. My "lessons" from Millie had given me a taste of what it was like to have a tongue inside my mouth, which was an experience I relished. The stranger's skill was something I hadn't expected. He pressed me to the window and all but seduced me, ravaging me with his silky and persistent tongue. I didn't want to enjoy the unexpected encounter. The length of his body crushed me, as heat poured through the layers of clothing, bringing the stinging shame of red to my cheeks.

His lips were on my neck, nibbling and sucking. "Oh, no…" I breathed.

"I should kidnap you…take you with me."

"Yes, I-I mean, no!" I had to push him away. Perhaps, after one more little kiss. "Ooommm…"

His lips were over mine with an urgency that should have shocked me to my senses. My arms wound around his neck, and I pressed myself to him, every nerve ending in my body suddenly craving his touch. But…we wore so many clothes…far too many.

"Sarah!" screamed a familiar voice in a lilting brogue. "You let her go!"

"Ouch! Jesus Christ!" he yelled. Millie had hit him

with her shillelagh. The walking stick thumped across his back. He flung his arm around, grabbing the weapon, and tossed it to the other side of the car. "I should shoot you for that, woman!"

"You leave that girl alone!"

"Irish bitch!"

"Oh, you haven't even seen me angry yet, mister."

The sound of a revolver discharging had our attention. Disheveled train robbers rushed through the car. "Run for it! There's an Army sergeant on board! We gotta get outta here, Brack!"

He stared at me. "It was nice meetin' you, Sarah." I was tongue-tied and paralyzed, my body buzzing with arousal. "I really should take you with me. I'd like to finish what we started."

A man in a torn corduroy jacket grabbed him. "Time to go!" They raced to the next car, disappearing from sight.

I gazed at where they'd gone, feeling numb and disappointed. I would never see that horrible man again…and that was…unfortunate.

Millie smiled crookedly. "That good, eh?"

"What?"

"The kiss."

"Oh, it was…oh, never mind. He stole my ring!"

"He would've taken a lot more than that if he had the chance."

I struggled to compose myself. "I need to fix my hair. I need…a nap."

She smiled knowingly. "I completely agree, my dear. A good lie down will set everything to rights."

After the drama at breakfast, I found myself in my camisole and drawers, reclining on the small bed, while the train continued to vibrate. We would be in Chicago the next morning.

Millie's hand was on my thigh. "You liked that man."

I nodded. "I did."

"It wouldn't be wise to tell Edmund about the kiss."

"I won't." Her hand slid into the waistband of my drawers. "Oh, Millie."

"I have to see something."

"What?"

"If you're as wet as I think you are." She'd found the juncture of my thighs. "And you are."

"I couldn't help it…oh…Millie…" Her fingers drove into the silky wetness of my pussy. I fell to the bed, as her thumb grazed my nub. "Oh, yes…"

"Would you have let him have you?"

"No." *Yes, yes, yes, yes, yes.*

"If you were alone, in private?"

I smiled, tingling where she touched me. "I…probably…but no, of course not. I can't. I'm…engaged."

She lowered my drawers, pulling them off. "For an outlaw he was a handsome one."

Curiosity had won out. "Tell me," I implored. "What does it look like?"

She clucked. "Oh, you dirty girl."

"Please, Millie. I want to know."

"You'll find out soon enough with your husband."

"But, you're supposed to be teaching me about all of that. How will I learn anything, if you don't teach it?"

She rummaged around inside a travel bag, bringing out a brush. The end is about this long, and the tip looks like the top of a peach."

I eyed the brush. "That long."

"Some are longer. Shaun's was crooked on the end."

"You mean bent?"

"Yes."

"Was he the only man you've ever slept with?" She gave me a look. "He wasn't, was he?" I scooted closer. "Oooh, do tell, Millie. Tell me everything."

"You're a strumpet, Sarah. You'll have to solve the mystery on your own." She unbuttoned her blouse. "We have an hour before dinner. Let's not waste it talking."

I bit my lip. "They get hard when they're near women, right?"

"If they're excited." She tossed the shirt aside and removed her corset. "Why?"

"I could feel his…thing."

"I'd be surprised if you didn't. You're a beautiful woman. I've seen the way men look at you."

"You have?"

"Yes, my dear. Wherever we go, you turn heads. You have for years."

"Oh." That was mildly shocking.

Her chemise, drawers, petticoat, and bustle ended up on a chair. "Now lay back like a good girl."

I shuddered at the tone in her voice. "What are we doing?"

"I'll start by pleasuring you with my tongue."

"That's a wonderful place to start."

"Then perhaps we can try something new."

"Like what?"

"A position where we fuck each other at the same time."

"How sinful."

"Oh, my dear. You have no idea."

Chapter Five

I kissed her, driving my tongue into her mouth. My encounter with the bandit had emboldened me, giving me a fearless edge and a desire to be more aggressive. I held her face, kissing her madly, biting on her lower lip and lapping at her mouth.

"What in heavens has gotten into you?"

"Oh! Millie! Touch my pussy…please."

"Let's get this off first." She grasped my camisole and pulled it over my head. "You have magnificent breasts."

"Yes, that's all good, but touch me." I grabbed her hand. "Touch my pussy."

"You're soaking wet."

"Oh! If you do that a little longer I'll explode. It won't take long. I'm almost there."

"I haven't even touched you, girl." She seemed slightly astounded.

The little I was receiving wasn't enough. I pounced on her, straddling a leg and began to grind myself against her. "Oh, Millie!" Something strange had happened to me that I couldn't quite explain. In my mind, I saw the bandit, and my body seemed to think her leg was his cock. I went mad rutting on it, nearly insane with want. "Oh! Oh, my goodness. I'm so sorry!" I threw my head back and moaned, while sparks flashed behind my eyelids and the world tumbled into rapture. I rode her shamelessly, enjoying the dwindling convulsions of my orgasm. I collapsed on the bed. "Ooohh…"

"You little tart."

"I'm sorry."

"My leg's all wet." Her hand was on my stomach. "You used me."

"I did," I laughed. "That was fun."

She smacked my thigh. "You've become an unruly student."

"It felt so good."

"You're more like your mother than you think."

I turned on my side, holding my head in the palm of my hand. "You keep saying that. What do you know?" I pushed her. "Tell me."

"I've heard stories about Africa. Orgies and things. There was a great white ape also. I think your mother knew him."

"Tarzan."

"You've heard of him then?"

"I met him. He's no ape. He's just a man."

"It's my turn now."

"But what else do you know?"

"Isn't an orgy bad enough?"

"That sounds exciting."

"Hold your tongue! Don't think things like that."

"I'm not allowed to do them, and now I can't even think about them? That's hardly fair." I giggled at her shocked expression.

"Lay back. I'm going to show you something new."

"Oooh...I love new things." She straddled me facing the other direction. Her thighs were on either side of my face, and her pussy was rapidly approaching. "What on earth are you doing?"

"I've heard of this. I want to try it." Her finger drove between the swollen lips of my pussy.

"Oh! It's so sensitive."

"And wet."

"Millie! I think I'm going to like this."

"It would surprise me if you didn't."

I giggled, "I'm not that debauched."

"I beg to differ." She lowered to my mound. "Suck me, you dirty girl."

"Oh…ooommmm…" I buried my face in her moist center, relishing the slightly musky aroma. Her tongue was in my pussy, and it felt slinky and wet. I buzzed all over again, my body humming a sensuous tune. I grasped the pillow and shoved it under my head to hold myself up. Then I tongued her and used my fingers, which rubbed over the distended lump of her clit.

"Oh, girl…that's so good."

I would have answered, but I was preoccupied, sucking gently on the scalloped edges of her labia. I rubbed her clit, and she moaned repeatedly; the soggy lump was even longer and harder now. She drove a finger into me, while using her thumb over my sensitive nub.

"Ooohh…Sarah…" She pressed herself to my mouth, wetting me thoroughly. "Oh, fuck me, girl! Fuck me!"

I wasn't the only one was aggressive that afternoon. I thought I might drown from the deluge that trickled down my throat. She was incredibly aroused. I hurtled towards another orgasm with a woman's vagina on my face. Grasping the soft flesh of her hips, I bucked mine up to feel her tongue over me. This happened repeatedly, until I gasped and moaned, my entire body trembling in a series of mini-shocks.

"Millie!" She sat on me, driving her cunt into my mouth. I thought I would surely suffocate in the sodden folds, but she groaned then, shuddering, rubbing her core hard and low.

"You dirty girl! Oohhh…" she gasped.

Exhausted, I collapsed against the pillow and sighed. "I like that position. It's mutually beneficial."

Millie giggled and fell to the bed, laying in the other direction. "It was marvelous. We should nap for a while. Then we have to get ready for dinner. That bandit aroused you."

"Mmmm…" *He sure did.* His image flitted through my consciousness. It was the last thing I remembered before drifting off to sleep.

Dinner that evening was a low-key affair. The topic of conversation had been the train robbers, who, by all estimates, had made off with more than twelve thousand dollars worth of money and jewelry. They were known as The Corbett Gang, led by Brack Corbett. He and his accomplices had robbed trains from Ohio to Iowa, extending as far West as Nevada. Lawmen and bounty hunters were in pursuit, including several Pinkerton detectives, who had boarded the train at a depot in Indiana. Millie and I had been asked questions about the incident, and I had given a statement, recollecting the sanitized version of events. I omitted kissing the handsome outlaw, and I buzzed every time I thought about it.

The next morning, after we had pulled into Chicago's Central Depot, I waited anxiously with Millie, while porters brought down our trunks. There was a lake breeze, which filled my senses with the smell of the ocean, but that was impossible because Lake Michigan was a fresh water lake. Perhaps, it was the vague aroma of fish that tricked me into imagining this.

"Sarah!" A man's voice called out above the din. Scores of people came and went.

"Edmund?"

"My love!" A tall man approached wearing a cutaway morning coat and ascot tie. His handsome visage was adorned by an enormous smile. "There you are. How was your trip?" He took my hand, kissing my gloved fingers.

"It's so good to see you, Edmund. We were robbed."

"What? I've hardly had time to read the papers. Are you all right?" His brows drew together. "You weren't harmed, were you?"

"No, but they made off with my engagement ring."

"I'm so sorry, my dear. How awful." He glanced at Millie, tipping his hat. "Mrs. Doyle. How are you?"

"I'm well, Mr. Lakewood, and you?"

"My man will bring the luggage. You're to go with him. I'm taking Sarah home. I want her to meet my sister, Isabelle." He smiled charmingly. "Come, my dear." He held out his arm, and I placed my hand on his wrist. "I've a new toy to show you. It's a Spider Phaeton."

I glanced at Millie. "I'll see you at the house."

The corners of her mouth turned down. I knew she was upset to be left with the bags, but she was my appointed travel companion, and I suspected my mother was paying her a wage. Edmund would never socialize with an employee, and, as we approached his sleek new conveyance, which only seated two, it would have been impossible to bring Millie along. I was caught up in the excitement of being alone with Edmund and the thrill of the city, which had fully recovered from the fire of 1871. The bustling metropolis held gravity defying skyscrapers, all within reach of the Mississippi and the Great Lakes. Immigrants and business tycoons alike found the jobs and opportunities to be plentiful, and they came in droves.

We arrived at an enormous redbrick structure with a bright red roof, just as the household staff filed out to greet us. I was taken aback slightly by the gesture, and, as Edmund held my hand, he helped me down from the lightly sprung carriage. I met the staff briefly, and then I was ushered into a marble entryway filled with a curving staircase.

"There she is," said a woman's voice. She glided towards me dressed in a Princess-line walking dress with a matching hat. "I've heard so much about you." She grasped my hands and brushed my face with her lips in greeting.

"Meet my sister, Isabelle. Isabelle, this is my fiancé, Sarah Collins."

"I know who she is, silly." She linked her arm through mine. "Let's have some tea. You must be exhausted. Sleeping on a train can't be restful."

The warm greeting astounded me. Edmund's parents had been stiff and reserved. I'd even wondered if they liked me at all. Isabelle was a delightful surprise, and from the friendly gleam in her eye, I suspected we might even be friends.

As she led me into the drawing room, she said, "I've heard about your ordeal. Those horrible train robbers! How exciting. You'll have to tell me everything. I do love a great adventure."

That evening, before dinner, Millie made her feelings known to me. "I know I shouldn't complain…"

"Oh, go on," I sighed. "I know you want to." I stuck another pin in my hair, hoping that this time, the wayward curl would stay in place.

"A Spider Phaeton? Why not a hansom cab? Who

drives a respectable young woman through town like that?"

"Oh, Millie."

"It's hardly appropriate. And there I was in a wagonette." Distaste marred her features. "I'm just as important as luggage."

I wrapped my arms around her, as she sat before a mirror. "Poorest dear. You're so sore tonight."

"Ay, that I am."

"I'm sorry."

"I shouldn't complain. I know my place. You've nothing to be sorry about."

"You'll always be special to me."

She snorted in reply. "We'll be late for dinner, if we don't hurry."

I slid my gloves on. "I like Isabelle. She has a marvelous sense of humor."

"She's a pretty woman."

My brows lifted. "Is she now?"

"Her figure is ravishing."

"It is." I eyed Millie carefully.

"Those breasts might just put us to shame."

I snatched my fan from the dresser, hitting her arm lightly. "Your observations are always so naughty."

"I appreciate the female form. Think of me as an art student admiring a sculpture."

I somehow doubted that was how she viewed women. "Go on."

"Her face…she's really lovely. That tiny nose and those lips…hm…" Her gaze drifted towards the wall. "She'll never be as beautiful as you…but…she's close."

"You think like a man."

"What?"

"When you look at women, you see them in a

sexual way, don't you?"

She shrugged. "I see beauty, Sarah."

"But you tingle in places, don't you? You think about them without clothes on. You imagine what their breasts feel like and how wet they are—"

"Now that's enough!" A pink shadow appeared over her cheeks. "Let's go down. We're already late."

I laughed, reaching for the doorknob.

Chapter Six

There were four of us at dinner, because Senator Lakewood and his wife were in Washington. We ate chicken tartar with broccolini and pecan pie for dessert. The conversation was light and fun and entirely unpretentious. Isabella, who had gone to school in England and traveled extensively, was charming and unique. Her opinions about Sitting Bull where shocking, as she sympathized with his plight. Her views on women being able to vote appealed to me, although Edmund disagreed passionately and interrupted her frequently. She had been engaged to a banker, but he had contracted consumption and died last year.

After dinner, Edmund kissed my cheek and bade me a good night. He was going to his club downtown. We were leaving for Omaha in the morning, and Millie and I would have the luxury of bathing in gas-heated water. As we undressed in an upstairs bathroom, I admired her figure, while she stood before a mirror, staring at her face.

"Millie. You really should marry again. You're much too young to let that body go to waste."

She lifted her hair over her head, securing it with a clip. "No. I'm done with that."

"Don't you want someone to take care of you? Don't you want children?"

"Your family takes care of me. I take care of you. Then one day, I'll take care of your children." She went to the tub, touching the water. "This is marvelous. Hurry up and get in."

"You first."

"No, my dear. You're the lady of the house. I'll wait

my turn."

I'd have to bathe quickly. I didn't want her to sit in cold water. "Fine." I hurried to remove my underthings, tossing them over the chair. A fire blazed not more than four feet away, warming the room. I got in and grabbed the soap, washing myself vigorously.

"You needn't rush."

I dunked under, my golden hair floating in the water. I used a chamomile and glycerin concoction, scrubbing my scalp aggressively. Millie rinsed the lengthy tresses, pouring water from a jug. I wrung the strands out, throwing them over a shoulder. "I'm done."

"You've not even relaxed."

"It doesn't matter. Get in. I'll sit by the fire and get the tangles out."

"You don't have to be so nice to me."

"Pish!" I dried off, feeling wondrously clean. "Let me know when you want me to rinse your hair."

She settled in the water. "Ooohh, this is wonderful."

"It is. Isn't it?" There was a knock on the door. "Yes?"

"Do you need more towels?" asked a female voice. It was Isabelle.

"We do."

"Might I come in?"

"Of course." Millie worked herself with the soap, unfazed by the interruption.

"Here are a few more." She placed them on a chair. "Isn't indoor plumbing a miracle of modern invention?"

"It is," I agreed. There was something entirely likeable about my future sister-in-law.

"I'll comb your hair, if you want." She wore a light blue dressing gown. "Edmund's gone to his club. It's only the girls in the house."

I was slightly disappointed that I had not been able to spend more time with my fiancé, but we would be on the train tomorrow, and the trip would afford us days together. "That would be nice, Isabelle." I sat before the fire.

She dragged a chair over and sat behind me. "It's like a private ladies only party."

"In the bathroom," quipped Millie.

"Should I get your hair?" I asked.

"Yes, please."

"I'll be back." Obtaining water from the sink, I poured it over Millie, rinsing the shampoo out. Then I sat by the fire, while Isabelle untangled my tresses.

"We should have a party," said Isabelle.

"We're not dressed, and my hair's wet."

"Edmund bought me a music box for Christmas. Let's listen to it."

"I love music boxes," said Millie.

"It's settled then. I'll go get it. I'll meet you in your room."

After she left, I glanced at Millie. "She's fun."

"I do approve of that one."

"I know you don't care for Edmund. I'm glad you like his sister."

"He's overbearing."

"Millie! You shouldn't be speaking so ill of my husband to be."

"I'm honest, Sarah. I won't lie to you."

"But you think all men are overbearing."

"Indeed."

I sighed. "So it doesn't matter who I marry. The

40

choices are bad and not so bad. I've settled for not so bad."

"You're a darling," she laughed. "You a silly girl."

I pointed a finger at her. "You're a seducer and a corrupter."

She gasped, "Sarah!"

"I speak the truth too. The things we've done together have changed me. I think about it all the time."

A peculiar light shone in her eye. "Think about what?"

"You know. The intimacies we've shared. The things we've done. I know how nice those things are. I really like our secret lessons."

"We must keep that quiet. You mustn't tell your husband. He wouldn't understand."

"It's our secret."

"Good."

"Ladies!" called Isabelle. "The party is ready."

I glanced at Millie. "When are you getting out of the tub?"

"Now."

"Good. I want to hear the music box."

"Go on. I'll be there in a moment."

I tossed the nightgown over my head. "Don't loiter or you'll miss all the fun."

In the bedroom, Isabelle handed me a champagne glass, which was a surprise. "Let's celebrate."

"What's the occasion?"

"Our adventure."

She would join us on the trip to California. "I've had adventure already." I sat on the bed.

"So I've heard." She sat next to me. "Your encounter with the train robber. What was that like?"

"He stole my engagement ring."

Her mouth fell open. "What a blackguard."

"He would've taken my locket, but I…talked him out of it."

"Rightly so. One should never underestimate the female power of persuasion. My mother always said I could talk myself out of a box."

There was something trustworthy about her, and my guard slipped by several degrees. "I had to kiss him."

"What?"

"He made me kiss him. He said he wouldn't take the locket, if I kissed him."

"What a scoundrel." She seemed thoughtful. "Was he pleasing to look at?"

"Yes."

"Was he well dressed?"

"No."

"Did he smell like horse manure?"

"No," I laughed. "He was clean. He was handsome in a sort of reckless way. He certainly wasn't someone I could take home to dinner."

"How was the kiss?"

"Very nice." I clamped my lips together, realizing that I had said too much. "I mean, he was…um…respectful."

"I hardly believe that. If given the time, he would've seduced you."

"Oh, no. I doubt that."

Her look was shrewd. "Has Edmund ever kissed you?"

"Of course."

"But not the mouth?"

"No."

"So he took liberties your fiancé wouldn't dare."

"Yes."

"And you enjoyed them."

Panic set in. "You think the worst of me now."

"Not at all. I like you, Sarah. You're spirited and lovely. You're charming and vivacious." Her smile fell. "I don't think Edmund would make you happy. He's pompous and droll."

"But you would say that. He's told me how you don't get along."

Her hand covered mine. "Let's not talk about Edmund. He's not worth a minute of my time. Have champagne. I'll wind up the music box."

Millie had joined us; her face was pink from the heated water. "What's that?"

"Champagne," said Isabelle. "Have a glass." A pretty melody filled the room. The bedroom was decorated in dark, heavily carved furniture and flower patterned wallpaper. Isabelle returned to the bed. "I love champagne." She downed her drink. "It makes me happy all over and do things I ought not."

I buzzed warmly. "What kinds of things?"

Her hand brushed against my knee. "Edmund will be gone for hours." I glanced at Millie, recognizing the look in her eye. Pinpricks of pleasure rushed up my spine. "I can keep secrets. I'm not an angel." Her touch on my leg grew bolder. She whispered, "This is what I miss about school. We used to play naughty games, and no one was the wiser. A woman isn't allowed to seek out pleasure. Even if she's married, she'll hardly find that." Her smile was coy. "But, if you have lady friends, and if things happen in private. No one needs to know. There's nothing wrong with friendship and pleasure."

"Millie," I said, feeling as if I'd just solved a riddle. "She's like you. She likes other women."

My chaperone nodded solemnly.

Chapter Seven

Isabelle smiled. "There's something about you I can't quite place, Sarah. I sensed it when we first met."

"My upbringing was unconventional."

"Yes, I've heard about Africa. Your family is adventurous. I've read all about your grandfather, Author Tennent. His travels in the jungle are well documented by the Royal Geographical Society. It's fascinating how he managed to live among those fearsome natives. You were there too and survived."

"You live with the Indians," I countered. "I've heard they can be just as dangerous as the *Azande*."

"They're not to be underestimated. The Calvary has its hands full keeping us safe. I've heard some things…unpleasant things I don't agree with, but…we can discuss them tomorrow." She smiled enticingly. "There are other matters I'd rather contend with." Her hand was on my thigh. "Wouldn't you say?"

The way the candlelight danced off her face made her look beguilingly beautiful. Her expression was predatory, yet seductive, which I found arousing. Men were hardly as forward, with the exception of that roguish train robber. But…that had been exciting, and just thinking about the way he had looked at me made the muscles in my pussy clench. The kiss we shared was singed in my memory, and it brought back every feeling, every nuance, including the way he had smelled. I could almost pick up the scent right now, leather and musk.

"She's thinking about something," murmured Isabelle. "She's flushed completely."

"That'd be the handsome outlaw," laughed Millie.

"What was the bandit's name? Brack? Ah…Brack Corbett. I think he stole more than her engagement ring."

"Oh, hush."

"Is that so? I've heard of the Corbett Gang. They're in the papers often."

"He…he was a scoundrel." I bit my lower lip, and Isabelle gazed at my mouth hungrily. "It doesn't matter. He can choke on the ring for all I care." Her hand massaged my thigh, which sent a rush of flutters to my tummy.

"We could play act, if you want," murmured Isabelle. "I could be the robber, and you could be my victim." Excitement suddenly animated her features. "That's it!" She got to her feet. "Stay here. I'll be back." She fled the room.

"What's gotten into her?"

"You didn't have to mention that train robber, Millie. It wasn't necessary."

"He's on your mind."

"No, he isn't."

"Oh, yes he is. I saw the way you kissed him. I was there."

"I had no choice."

"Ha!"

I squared my shoulders. "Are you jealous?"

"Of gutter trash?" She snorted. "No."

"I think you are."

"I can't leave you alone, ever. I turn my back, and you're being molested. You weren't putting up much of a fight."

"Stop judging me, Millie. You're one to talk about molesting. What about the first time you tried to—" My breath caught in my throat. In the doorway stood

Isabelle dressed in trousers, boots, and an overcoat. There was a wide-brim hat on her head. "Good lord."

She held a revolver; the weapon was pointed at me. "Don't worry. It's not loaded."

Millie's hand went to her mouth. "Oh, what a sight," she laughed.

"What on earth are you doing?" It was then that I realized I adored Isabelle. She was as spirited and fearless as I wished to be. Either that, or she had completely lost her marbles. "Why, I never..."

"This here is a train robbery." Her voice was low and gravelly. Hand over your money and jewelry." She pointed the gun at me. "Go on, young lady. I know you're hiding your valuables. Remove that dress." Millie shook her head, clearly entertained. "I won't be sayin' it again." It sounded as if she were trying to accent her voice as well.

Seeing the hat and the gun brought back a flood of naughty memories. I decided to play along. "I won't, you scoundrel!"

She stalked towards me, her boots sounding hollow on the wooden floor. "Take off that dress or I'll rip it from you. Don't think I won't."

"But...that's unseemly."

"I don't care nothin' about decorum. All I want is what you're hiding on your person. Take 'em off."

"She's a wonderful train robber," quipped Millie.

Isabelle pivoted, pointing the gun at her. "You hush, woman! You'll be next."

She held up her hands in defense. "Oh, my goodness gracious. You're truly the worst sort of train robber. You should be ashamed of yourself for terrorizing the regular folk."

"Just sit there, and be quiet." The gun was pointed

at me again. "Take 'em off, little lady. I won't say it again."

"You're a big, mean man."

"Off. Now!" Her tone was low and threatening.

"Oh, fine." I lifted the nightgown over my head, tossing it on the floor. "Are you happy?"

"Where are you hiding your valuables?"

"Nowhere, as you can see."

"Those breasts are sinful, Miss."

"Really?"

"You're committing several crimes with those."

I crossed my arms over my chest, laughing, "You don't say."

"I'll have to examine you thoroughly to find what I'm looking for. Lay on the bed."

"I'm being robbed! Help!"

Isabelle's eyes flew wide. "Shush! Not so loud!" Her regular voice had returned. "The servants will come running." Laughter filled the room. The situation was ridiculous, yet highly diverting. She cleared her throat. "Now, do as I ask, and no one will get hurt."

I lay on the bed, my legs dangling off the end. "Oh, fine. Search me, you filthy bandit."

Isabelle approached, a hint of a smile playing around her lips. "You're not scared enough of me, I'm afraid. I better rectify that."

"I have the strength of the Lord to fortify me. I fear nothing with Him on my side." A peal of laughter escaped Millie.

"You'll be screaming His name when I'm done with you." I trembled and buzzed everywhere. It felt as if all my nerve endings had risen, saluting her. The slight breeze from the partially open window hardened my nipples, the pink buds pointing upwards. She leaned

48

over me, her face half hidden by the hat. "What's your name?"

"S-Sarah."

"You're a pretty virgin." She thought for a moment. "Are you a virgin?"

"I think…so."

"Why the hesitation?"

"I'm not sure."

"You ever have a penis in you?"

"No, ma'am, I mean, sir."

"Then you're a virgin."

"I guess I am."

"Do you touch yourself?"

"That's none of your business." The gun was pointed at me. I trembled slightly, thinking that, if it were loaded, it would indeed be dangerous. "I…might've."

"I see." She placed the weapon on the bed. "I'll need to search you, Miss. Now, you lay nice and still for me, and no one will get hurt."

"But…w-what's your name?"

Isabelle smiled. "I'm Brack Corbett. At your service."

"You are a scoundrel," I breathed.

"You don't know the half." I felt flushed from my waist up, the heat searing me. Dampness registered in my pussy, and, as she leaned over me, I began to shiver. Her hand was on my belly. "You're quivering."

"Only my husband should touch me." My voice was hardly above a whisper.

"He ain't here to recue you." She tossed the hat to the floor. Her hair was held back in a ponytail. "Now then. I'm gonna have to check every nook and cranny for those jewels. You better not move."

Thinking of her as the lusty train robber had an unusual effect on me. I vibrated with arousal, my nerve endings screaming with the possibility of pleasure. Her hand was on my tummy, and the gentleness of the touch had me arching my back slightly, thrusting my breasts out, the milky globes spilling across my ribcage. Millie sat in a chair, not more than five feet away; her amusement was tempered with interest.

"You're lovely," breathed Isabelle. She'd used her own voice. "I should be jealous." Our eyes met, and passion flared. "There's something so beautiful about the female body. It's a shame to have to hide all of this under layers and layers of clothes." She grasped my breasts, pressing them together. "I'm gonna have to check these carefully, ma'am," she rasped in her play voice. "These look suspicious."

She rubbed her face against my burning flesh, her tongue flicking over a nipple. "Oh!" I nearly sprang off the bed from the feel of my firm little buds in her mouth. My eyes rolled into my head, my mouth opening, as my lips formed an O. I gratefully succumbed to what was happening to me. Her face was soft, so unlike how the bandit had felt. As she suckled, I envisioned Brack's lips on me. I could almost feel the roughness of his beard. "Oh," I breathed. "You're a bad...bad bandit."

Her hand skimmed lower, drifting to my mound. "You're very wet ma'am. I've heard ladies like to hide things here. I'm gonna have to check you carefully."

My clitoris was in such a state, that, when she pressed against it, I could feel it shifting. "Brack!" The sound of his name on my lips, uttered in a moment of sexual excitement, was scandalizing.

"Say my name again," she grated.

I tossed my head from side to side. "Oh, no, no, no, no."

"I think you're hiding something, Miss. I don't think it's jewels either."

Chapter Eight

I lifted my head off the bed to stare at her. I caught sight of Millie on the chair. Her nightgown was bunched around her knees, and her hand was in her crotch, presumably fingering the inner recesses of her cunt. Knowing that we had affected her in this manner added yet another level of wantonness to this already depraved scene.

"Say my name again!" Her finger slid between swollen lips, which were so bloated, they pressed together.

Whatever resistance I had been able to maintain melted. "Brack..."

"That's it. Now you're mine." She sat up quickly, discarding her jacket. "It sure is hot in here." She continued to sound low and raspy, trying to emulate a man. "Now spread those pretty legs, lady. I'm gonna have to investigate every little bit of what you got here."

"Oh, my...goodness..."

She blew gently across my skin, the coldness of the effect highlighting how wet I had become. As her tongue skimmed over my nub, her hands slid up my chest, reaching for my breasts. My nipples were rolled and pinched, the sensations leaving me weak and gasping. My eyes were closed, and all I could think about was the train robber. If we had been alone, would things have gone this far? It was a shame that I would never see him again. His sort ended up shot by the law or hung by the courts.

But...none of that mattered now. "Oh, Brack..."

"I think you're lying to me, lady. I think you're hiding something deep inside here. I'm gonna get to the bottom of it."

If I hadn't been so aroused, the sound of her voice would have been amusing and her words even more so. The situation was ridiculous, but my body's reaction to her touch wasn't a joke. We had taken a deliciously naughty path from which none of us wanted to deviate. Firm fingers drove through the silky wetness of my pussy, sinking in deeply. She wiggled them, twisting around and massaging me intimately. With a skill that matched Millie's, her tongue prodded, pushing and manipulating my clit, creating a burst of tiny flitters that fanned out from my core.

"Brack!"

The game was now over. The attention she paid my lower anatomy had grown very serious indeed. She was fully invested in pleasuring me, her fingers rubbing and moving in my tight tunnel. I touched her scalp, urging her on. I began to pant, my chest rising and falling, as if I had just dashed out of the way of a moving carriage.

"Oh-OH! Oh, my…goodness…gracious…" I caught a glimpse of Millie, slumped against the chair, working her cunt feverishly. She was nearing her peak. "Oh, you bad bandit. Bad…"

Isabelle tried to push three fingers into me, but the snugness of the orifice wouldn't allow it, so she continued with two, reaming me thoroughly. I wanted to hold off the orgasm for a few minutes longer, but my body had other ideas. I arched my back, moaning uncontrollably.

"Brack! Oh, God, Brack!"

My nerve endings burst wide open like Chinese fireworks on the Fourth of July. I grasped the bedspread, clutching the material, while I convulsed helplessly, the springs creaking loudly.

"Oh, bless…me…" moaned Millie, in the clutches of her own release.

When I peaked at the room, I saw my soon to be sister-in-law. "You're so…" Words failed me.

She grinned, removing the man's shirt, exposing a chest filled with pale, lovely breasts. "This will be our dirty little secret."

"Now you sound like Millie."

"I wondered about you."

I sat up, tossing thick strands of blonde hair over my shoulder. "How?"

"I have a sense about people. I wondered if you'd be fun."

Overwhelmed by emotion and feeling utterly at peace, I flung my arms around her, burrowing my face in her neck. "From this day forward, you're my sister. I won't think of you as any less."

"I was prepared to hate you. I've met some of my brother's other suitors, and they were awful. I thought you'd be just the same. I'm so glad I was wrong."

My hands cupped her breasts. "It's my turn. I want to make you scream my name when you…find your pleasure."

Her grin was enormous. "Then I better get these pants off."

"They look ridiculous on you, by the way."

"I've never had such fun." She kicked the trousers free, knocking the revolver to the floor, where it discharged. The sound of the weapon firing at such proximity had my ears popping painfully. Acrid smoke filled the room.

"Dear Lord in heaven!" shouted Millie. "That wasn't empty at all! We could've been killed!"

I met Isabelle's horrified gaze. "Oh, my God," she

uttered. "I…oh, God. I thought I took the bullets out."

"Maybe there was one left?"

"I…oh, dear. Edmund always said women and guns don't mix."

I slid from the bed. "There's a hole in the wall now."

"I'll shove some paper in it, and it'll be good as new," laughed Isabelle.

She had pointed the gun at Millie and I repeatedly. We could have been shot! A naughty idea formed. "You deserve a spanking for that, Isabelle. That was very stupid. Stupid girls should be punished."

Millie nodded enthusiastically. "At least. I'd belt her myself, if I could."

"That's a capital idea!" I snatched the trousers off the floor, pulling the leather belt free. "You have to be punished. You almost killed me."

Isabelle sobered. "You're right." She glanced at the belt. "What exactly are you going to do with that?"

"Bend over the bed." I snapped the leather strap against my hand, producing a whacking sound. "Ouch!" It stung. I would have to employ a level of control when hitting Isabelle. I didn't want to injure her. Or did I?

"Do as she says, girl," said Millie. "Bend over the bed. Show us that pretty bottom."

"Well, this I hadn't foreseen. But…I suppose I could play along."

"You will," I asserted. "Get over the bed. Now!"

"I do deserve it, for almost shooting you."

"Now!"

"Fine!" She leaned over the bed, her rounded bottom in the air.

"How hard should I hit her, Millie?"

"Start light. Work your way up from there."

"Oh," she breathed. "You two are…naughty."

"You're a careless sister-in-law. You almost killed me. Now prepare to be punished."

Millie took her nightgown off, dropping the garment on the floor. She picked up the wide-brim hat and placed it on her head. There was something sexy about a naked woman with only a hat on. "What are you waiting for? That ass is ripe for spanking."

"But first," I pulled Isabelle's boots off, "I'm wearing these."

"You're both ridiculous," she laughed.

"Shush!" I smacked her with the end of the belt, the sound echoing.

"Oh! Oh, you—"

"Smack!"

"Oh! That hurts!"

"Hit her harder."

My grin was saucy, and I knew it. "I should hit her harder, shouldn't I?"

"The woman almost killed you. She deserves a beating, if you ask me."

"Oh, Millie. What do I do? I've never done this before." I couldn't get over the hat. It looked bizarre on her, especially with her large breasts jutting.

"Give me the belt." She held out her hand. "I'll show you what to do."

"Don't go too crazy." There was something in her look that worried me.

Her smile was enigmatic. "Give me the belt, Sarah."

"Oh, all right, but I'm watching you. Don't take it too far."

"Be a good girl, and sit."

"I'm waiting," said Isabelle. "Are you going to

punish me or not?"

"Touch her pussy. Tell me if she's wet."

I slid a hand along the curves of her ass to the back of her thigh. She felt so soft, so supple. Her pussy was hidden behind glossy curls, and, as my fingers sought her opening, wetness appeared on my hand. "She's plenty wet."

"Good. Then we can begin." She lifted the belt, hitting Isabelle with the leather strip.

"Ouch!"

"That's it." She struck her again.

"Oh!"

If I had been worried that Millie would abuse my soon to be sister-in-law, my concern was for naught. She drew the belt back, letting it snap against her pale skin creating streaks of pink. Soon her bottom was crisscrossed with red. Isabelle gasped with each hit, flinching slightly, but her face betrayed her. It seemed as if the pain morphed almost instantly into pleasure.

"You should hit her harder, Millie."

"That's what I was thinking." She snapped at her thighs as well, producing several angry red marks.

"I didn't know this could be pleasurable." Isabelle wasn't the only one aroused. My pussy throbbed distractingly; so much so, I pushed my fingers into the soggy snatch, manipulating it feverishly. "This is...wicked."

"Smack!"

"Ouch! Ooohhh..."

Millie continued to assault the rounded buttocks, leaving over-lapping lines of redness. The harder she hit her, the louder Isabelle moaned. Her vocal, guttural pleasure was punctuated by loud snapping.

"How wet is she now?"

I slid my hand between her legs. "Very wet."

"Lick her."

"What?"

"You heard me. Get between her legs and lick her."

I nearly achieved orgasm, right then and there. It took a full minute to compose myself, urging my body to recede from the edge. "Yes, Millie." I slid from the bed, approaching Isabelle's sexy bottom. I buried my face between her cheeks, holding her thighs apart, until I had access to her slit. I ran my tongue over the glistening lips of her labia.

"Oh, my God," she groaned. "Oh, my…holy…God…"

She smelled pungently of arousal, the creamy fluid pooling at the edges of her womanhood. "Should I do more?"

"Lick her while I hit."

Alarm raced through me. "You won't hit me, will you?"

"Not unless you want me to."

"Millie!"

She grinned. "Suck that pussy, Sarah. Do it."

"Yes ma'am." I applied my tongue, pushing further into her moist opening.

"Smack!"

"Ouch!"

I laved her aggressively, wiping away excessive amounts of honeyed nectar. My face was wet with her juices, and, as Millie continued to hit her, she dripped even more.

"Oh, dear Lord in heaven!"

"Smack!"

"Oh, goodness. I…can't help it! Oooh…"

Isabelle shuddered, her pussy gushing; so much so,

I worried she had peed herself. A torrent of water poured down her inner thighs. "What on earth!"

"Oh, God," she groaned. "Ohhh…you…dirty…women…"

I glanced at Milly. "What was that?"

"It happens to some women. It's not urine, if that's what you're worrying about."

"I see." This had been an education, the play-acting, the whipping, and now a gushing pussy. "Oh, my."

"I can't believe I did that." She sounded exhausted. "That was incredible. It was…so good. I've never…I've never experienced it so good."

"We could do it again," I suggested. My pussy throbbed. An orgasm waited patiently on the horizon.

Millie glanced at me, smiling slightly. "This could be a long night."

Chapter Nine

We had indulged ourselves for hours, taking a bath afterwards, washing away the evidence of our debauchery. By morning, the three of us were the best of friends, dressing together, laughing, and packing as quickly as we could. The trunks were taken down and transported to the train station.

Edmund waited at the foot of the stairs, looking fresh and dapper in a knee-length topcoat with a velvet collar. "Ladies, the train won't wait for us."

"I know, brother dear," trilled Isabelle. "We're coming!"

Edmund took my hand, kissing my glove. "You look ravishing, my love. You've got color on your cheeks."

"Thank you." *And how did you come by that color, Sarah? Well, I spent the night with my face buried between a woman's thighs, that's how.* "It's a lovely day, isn't it?" *If only you knew what I had done to your sister…repeatedly.*

"A lovely day to begin a journey."

"Look at the time. Haste! Haste!" called Isabelle, heading out the door. "Make haste!"

We rushed to the station, fighting our way through the traffic. Skyscrapers were all the rage; the building boom was in full swing. Workmen on scaffolding labored over heavy-looking masonry. Chicago was hemmed in by the lake and the rail yards; therefore, the only way to grow was up. The station was awash with businessmen, families with children, and porters.

Piercing whistles announced the imminent arrival of another locomotive. Whitish steam from various chimneys filled the air. We settled in a well-appointed parlor car, relaxing in the over-sized seats. Edmund ordered a brandy, and I had lemonade with the ladies. As the train jerked forward, the screech of the wheels was deafening.

Once we were on our way, Edmund asked, "What did you do last night?" I nearly choked on the lemonade.

"We had a marvelous time together." Isabelle winked at me. "Didn't we, Sarah?"

"Oh, most certainly."

"Doing what exactly?"

"Listening to the music box."

"It's a miracle it still works. It's been dropped more times than I can count."

"It works just fine. Every note was in tune."

As we engaged in small talk, my mind wandered, thinking about Isabelle dressed in men's clothing and pretending to be a train robber. Then I recalled the actual robbery, and how handsome the bandit had been. I replayed every second of the encounter, my stomach fluttering and trembling with pleasure.

An hour later, Millie handed me a newspaper. "This might interest you."

"Thank you."

The headline read: *The Corbett Gang Strikes Again! On the morning of July 2, 1880, the gang, consisting of Brack Corbett, Buck Bass, and Jimmy McCarty, set its sights on the B&O Railroad. After boarding the train in Willard, Ohio, the gentlemen robbers were brash and bold, taking more then twelve thousand dollars in cash and jewelry. The only injury reported was the train's brakeman, Clint Aldridge, who was wounded in the arm by a stray bullet. U.S. Marshall Robert Blain has—"*

"What are you reading, my dear?"

I glanced at Edmund, seeing a man with a slightly impassive expression. "My train robbery."

"Why trouble yourself with bad memories? I'll buy you another engagement ring. You won't be without one for long."

That had been the last thing on my mind. "Thank you, Edmund. That's very kind of you."

"Think nothing of it, sweetness." His attention returned to a book he was reading.

Ever since our engagement, he had become curt and standoffish. It wasn't that long ago that he had stopped the carriage in the middle of a thoroughfare, dashed into a flower shop, and returned with a bushel of roses. He had been wildly romantic and delightfully impulsive, although he had never kissed me properly. He would hold my hand under the table at dinner and write me love notes. That had all changed the night he had gotten down on one knee and proposed. It was almost as if the effort it took to win me had exhausted him. The quest was over, and now there was nothing to do but wait for the wedding.

After dinner, Millie, Isabelle, and I changed into our dressing gowns and settled in the sleeping car. Edmund had joined the men for drinks in the dining car. I sat on the bed, with one leg tucked under, braiding my hair.

"Where do you think you'll go on your honeymoon?" asked Isabelle.

"San Francisco."

"Oh, marvelous. I've been there before. The bay is gorgeous."

"Maybe we'll settle there."

"I would. Being near the ocean is wonderful. Please

don't stay in Sacramento."

"My parents have a farm with horses. My father breeds them." It had been oppressively hot today, and the upper portions of the windows were open. Something suddenly whizzed over our heads, embedding in the wood paneling on the other side of the wall with a loud thunk. "What was that?" It looked like an arrow with black and white feathers on the end.

"Oh, my God!" screamed Isabelle. "Indians!"

"Don't panic!" said Millie. "Get down. Sit on the floor."

"Are we under attack?"

"They shoot at trains often," said Isabelle. "They hate us for being here. We've taken so much of their land."

"Should I be worried?"

Isabelle touched my shoulder. "It's a stray arrow. It happens from time to time."

The whistle began to sound, blaring over and over, the lights flickering, and then the floor shuddered violently, throwing us to the other side of the car. The sound of steel grating and wood popping roared through my consciousness. I reached for Millie, who had begun screaming.

"We're bloody going to die! It's crashing!"

I grabbed the steel post of the bed. "Hold on!" The sleeping car began to shift, tilting precariously to the left. The sound of glass shattering forced my head down, and I squeezed my eyes shut to protect them. Something nicked my forehead and wetness trickled down my cheek.

"Mother of God!" screamed Isabelle. "Grab something!"

"Millie!"

"I'm fine! Hold on! Don't let go!"

The car was off its track, careening forward and angling to the left. It smelled like a bonfire; wood was burning, but not in our car. An enormous blast shook us, and the remaining windows imploded, shooting out shards of glass. Isabelle screamed, and I joined her, knowing my life was about to end. I gripped the bottom of the bed, the metal shaking precariously. If the pole came loose, I would be tossed around like a sack of potatoes. The feeling of falling suddenly brought a fresh wave of terror. The entire car shifted, keeling, ready to hit the ground.

"The saints preserve us!" shouted Millie. "Our Lord, our father! Our Lord in heaven! Our Lord—"

A gigantic boom registered, followed by violent shuddering, as the car hit the ground and continued to move, the force of motion propelling it forward in a straight line. The sounds of screams echoed, as fellow passengers dealt with the disaster. Dirt and grime hit my face, the aroma of grass and weeds filling my lungs. The landing had jarred me, wrenching my arm. Pain throbbed from my elbow to my wrist.

"Sarah!" It was Millie's voice.

"I'm here!" We continued to move, a fresh spray of dirt flying at me. Smoke filled the car, hindering visibility.

"Isabelle?"

"Goddammit!"

I smiled. She was just fine. "Is everyone all right?"

"When is this damn thing stopping?" asked Isabelle. "I've had enough now!"

Another loud boom was followed by a cacophony of screams. The passengers were suffering in the derailment, and many lives would be lost. Where was

Edmund? He'd been in the dining car in the middle of the train. Our car was towards the rear. Then I heard something that sent a chill down my spine. There were a series of shrieks and whoops that had nothing to do with the passengers or the train derailing. The sound reverberated on all sides, punctuated by the continuing roar of splintering wood, shattering glass, and metal grating. When the car finally skidded to a halt, I let go of the bottom of the bed and held my arm, wincing. It throbbed unpleasantly, the feeling centered near my wrist. I prayed it wasn't broken.

"Millie!"

"I'm here. Can you stand?"

"Y-yes."

"Let's find a way out." Her hands were on my shoulders. "Up with you."

"I'm not wearing shoes."

"I'm not either. It doesn't matter."

"Shit!" spat Isabelle. "Shit! Shit! Shit!"

"Are you hurt?" I asked.

"Shit on all of this! Goddamn shit on a stick!"

"I think she's fine," I muttered. Once the smoke had cleared, it was easier to see, but fires burned in another part of the train.

"Let's get out on the end," said Millie. "We've separated from the other car."

I stepped on something sharp. "Ouch!"

"Be careful. There's glass everywhere."

"Those Goddamned Indians did this!" hissed Isabelle. "They crashed the train! Now we'll be kidnapped and raped."

"Let's deal with one thing at a time," said Millie. She grabbed me. "Lord, girl. Your face is a mess."

"Glass got me." She held my arm. "Ouch!"

"Is it broken?"

"I don't know." I sounded miserable.

We made our way towards the opening in the back of the car, as strange whoops and shrieks froze my blood. Hollow sounding thunks and pomphs pinged around us, as arrows lodged in the wood.

"Oh, great. The goddamned Indians," muttered Isabelle.

We managed to climb down from the wreckage. Rocks dug into the bottoms of my feet. Gazing towards the front portion of the train, I knew I would never forget this disaster. The cars had landed haphazardly on their sides; some had piled up on one another. Plumes of smoke filled the sky, with intermittent fireballs blazing with red and yellow flames. It looked like a scene from Dante's *Inferno*. There were bodies scattered around us; some had burned, while others had fallen victim to arrows lodged in their chests, protruding grotesquely. This was indeed hell.

Something viselike grabbed the back of my head, tangling in my hair, and forcing my gaze upwards. In those breathless and unbelievable seconds, I saw the face of a man, his dark eyes flashing with hunger, lust, and triumph. I had just met the devil. I was in his clutches…and then I saw nothing, as my overwrought senses succumbed to merciful blackness.

Chapter Ten

I don't know how long I had been slung over the backside of a horse, but when I began to realize my situation, it was still the dead of night, and I was most assuredly in the clutches of a devil Indian. I wore my nightgown and nothing else, my hair falling in my face. The sound of female crying forced my head up. Millie sat on the next horse; her rider was fearsome to behold, wearing only a breechcloth and fringed leggings. My kidnapper wore the same type of leather over his legs. There were no stirrups and no saddles, only rope for a bridal.

I struggled to move, because I ached in this position. Sensing that I had woken, my kidnapper reached for me with impossible strength, dragging me to him. I straddled the horse, the abundance of material on my nightgown allowing for this, but now the bottom portion of my legs were bare. I was able to see what was happening around me. Isabelle and Millie were on other horses, in the clutches of dark skinned and determined Indians. Glancing back, I caught sight of smoke, the evidence of the train wreck we had left behind.

Then I made the mistake of looking at the man who held me. My long, blonde hair lashed us both, yet his was equally long and braided on each side. His face was clean-shaven, his cheekbones implausibly high, his nose gracefully straight, and those eyes…

…oh, dear…

They seemed to burn through me, leaving a scorching hole on the other side of my head. I'd never been this close to a man before, and I could feel the heat of his naked chest through the sheer cotton gown. His arms tightened around me, and I grimaced. My arm throbbed, reminding me of the horrors of the train wreck and how we should have all died. He seemed to sense my discomfort, lessening his grip. We rode for another hour, until the horses slowed, trotting side by side.

The Indians spoke, the language sounding bizarre and guttural. It seemed as if they were deciding on something, and there was a slight disagreement. My rider tensed, his anger evident in the clipped tones he uttered. The second rider capitulated, slowing even more. We stopped a short while later. My kidnapper dismounted, reaching for me. I glanced at Millie. Her face was smudged with coal.

"Glad you're finally awake, Sarah."

"And what a wonderful thing to wake up to," I grumbled.

"Oh, honey. You better brace yourself. If you can get your soul to leave your body, I'd do it now."

What had she meant by *that*?

I slid from the horse and straight into the heathen's arms, moaning in pain. "Ouch." He held my arm, although I tried to snatch it back. His fingers pressed into my wrist, working their way to my elbow. It hurt where he touched me, but it wasn't unbearable. He seemed to be ascertaining the extent of my injury, and, when he had assured himself it was nothing significant, he let me go.

"Don't touch me!" Isabelle smacked her rider, hitting him across the face. He seemed stunned by her behavior, stepping back a foot.

My rider laughed then, the sound deep and rumbling. I glanced at him, glowering and wishing him dead. His humor continued as he stared at me, taking in the unruly mess of hair, my bloodstained face, and God only knows what. How was I supposed to know what this Indian was thinking? Then he shocked me.

"You're not hurt."

"W-what?" I could understand him!

"Your arm. It's not broken."

"You speak English?"

There was something forbidden and mysterious in that smile. "A little. It's good to speak the language of your enemy." His accent was pronounced.

"I'm not your enemy. I'm a traveler whose train you've sabotaged. You killed so many people. Take me back this instant!" Why was he smiling like that?

"Do they all speak English?" asked Millie.

"No," the Indian said. "Just me."

His tone was pleasing, and so were his features, which bothered me immensely. That chest…naked…hairless…contoured with muscles…but I wasn't going to think about that. I wasn't even going to look at it anymore. "What's your name?"

His smile revealed straight, ivory teeth. "Laughing Hawk."

"The hell with this!" spat Isabelle. She'd gotten on a horse, grimacing. "If you think I'm staying to be raped and murdered, you got another thing coming. Her heels dug into the mare's flank. "Ha!" she shouted, sending the animal into an all out gallop. The hooves flung dirt, as she thundered in the other direction. I stared at her with my mouth open, amazed and in awe.

One of the Indians laughed, smirking at his friend. Then he jumped on Millie's horse and followed Isabelle, who hadn't looked back. I doubted her escape would last much longer, yet I envied her spunk and courage. Distracted as we were with their sudden departure, Millie took the opportunity to dash into the field, quickly being swallowed by wild corn, which reached nine feet into the air. Her captor, who grinned broadly at Laughing Hawk, followed her leisurely, sauntering into the foliage, as if he were on a Sunday stroll. My sister-in-law and my chaperone had deserted me! Feeling useless and abandoned, I too darted into the corn, but strong hands grabbed at my nightgown, the sound of fabric ripping filling my ears.

"No!"

"You can fight, pretty woman. I don't mind."

"Ooh! Stop that!" I struggled to gain my freedom, my arm suddenly aching. "Ouch!" I dropped to my knees, hopelessness seeping into my bones, and began to cry. I rocked back and forth, uttering, "I can't believe this is happening. I can't believe this is happening." I had just survived a horrific train crash that had probably killed scores of people, and now I was about to be brutalized by a heathen. A sense of despair had me shivering. His arms went around me. "No!"

I was forced on my knees, my nightgown thrown over my back, exposing buttocks and thighs. I wasn't able to form a coherent thought before something hard pressed against my pussy, demanding entrance. Never having had anything larger than two fingers inside of me, I screamed when he thrust, burying his tool to the balls.

"Stop it, you pig!"

He grunted, thrusting; the feeling was not entirely unpleasant, but I wasn't aroused in the least. My fingernails were dirty from the soil and weeds I gripped to steady myself. He was insistent and brutal, hammering my tight sheath, over and over, until he groaned, stiffening. Tears fell blinding me, the dam bursting, and I cried, while the brute enjoyed the virginity he had stolen. When he let me go, I collapsed to the ground in utter despair, feeling used and violated. I just wanted to lie there and die from shame, but it wasn't to be.

He grabbed me, dragging me to my feet, and we walked to where his horse was. "Sit," he barked. I sank to the ground, miserable and trembling.

Wetness slid down my inner thighs, a reminder of what had happened to me. I would curse God, if I fell pregnant. He busied himself making a fire, while in the distance I heard a woman scream. It was either Millie or Isabelle. They were experiencing exactly what had happened to me, or perhaps something even worse, but I doubted that was possible. There was a slight coolness to the air, but the fire quickly remedied this, the blaze burning brightly. Laughing Hawk untied a rolled up blanket that was attached to his horse, tossing it on the ground.

"Come with me." He held out his hand.

"No."

"You have blood on your face."

"What do I care?"

He grabbed me, pulling me to my feet and dragged me to a line of trees. I stumbled barefoot towards the sound of water. At the river's edge, he tore off a portion of my nightgown and dunked the material, ringing it out. "Hold still." He wiped my face, but the rag quickly dirtied. I hadn't realized I had bled so badly. I touched my forehead, feeling the wound.

"Take your clothes off."

I bristled. "I will not." He looked at me in such a way that I knew, if I disobeyed, he would shred the garment. Then I would be left with nothing to wear. "Oh, fine!" I whipped it over my head. "Are you happy now?"

"Wash. There's too much blood."

The water was cold, but it felt wonderful. It wasn't deeper than two feet, so I sat, freezing, and rinsed my face. He stood and watched, predatory and formidable. I hadn't had time to process the fact that this heathen stole my virginity. If I thought about it, I would surely cry again. My hand slid to my abused pussy, washing away the evidence of his seed. I stood and wrung out my hair, casting him a hateful glance. The coldness of the air had me shivering.

"Are you happy?"

His dark eyes roamed from the top of my head to my face. From there he went to my breasts, lingering for a long moment before lowering to my stomach and beyond. Lust flared in his look, and the front of his breechcloth began to rise.

Oh, great. He's going to…do it to me again.

"Come here." Having no choice, I stepped from the stream. He took the cloth, dabbing my forehead and examining the wound carefully. "Hold this firmly to stop the bleeding."

"Give me my nightgown."

"No."

Oh! You disgusting pig!

He led me up the small embankment through the trees. Stars like diamonds glimmered over our heads, a decorative curtain for the moon, which was partially hidden behind wispy clouds. When we reached the fire, I sat on the blanket, wet and shivering. I glared at my captor, wishing a snake would bite him, but then I panicked, worrying the same might happen to me. To my growing horror, he began to remove his clothing; the leather was decorated with paint and beads. His buckskin leggings were untied and tossed to the ground. When he was naked, an image of muscled perfection approached, and I moved to the edge of the blanket. He reached out touching my hair, and I slapped his wrist away. He laughed at that, the sound rumbling in his chest, and then he dragged me to him, forcing me to sit on his lap.

"No!" At that moment, two different sets of female screams sounded, from opposite directions. "You horrible Indians. Horrible."

"Your people have killed mine. You shoot children. You rape women. You burn villages. You're the enemy." Anger flared in his look.

"I didn't do it! I'm from England! I was born in Africa! I've never even been to America before."

His face was in my neck. "You're white. You're the enemy."

"That's a rather slim way of classifying things, isn't it?"

"What do you mean?"

"It's like saying all white people are bad."

"You say all Indians are bad."

"No…I don't." But I had. I had thought of them all as murdering, scalping heathens. "You derailed the train. You killed so many people. My fiancé is probably dead." Tears blurred my vision.

"You're in our land. We stopped the metal beast. Maybe no more will come now. Today has been a great victory for my people. Now we celebrate."

"You're horrible. You took my virginity." He brushed away a tear, and I was mildly surprised by this show of compassion. "You've no right to touch me."

His gaze settled on my lips, and I perceived his intentions. "No!"

Strong hands gripped my face, holding me immobile, as an aggressive tongue plunged into my mouth, despite my protests. His desire to subdue me had turned into a battle, because I fought him, pushing and struggling, trying to escape those insistent lips. The cock beneath me was rock hard and ready to assault my virgin pussy...again. Determination renewed my struggle, and I redoubled my efforts to fight him off, biting him.

"Ach!" He shoved me to the blanket, his face twisted in anger. There was blood on his lip. "You'll answer for that." I lifted my knees, preparing to kick him away, but he brushed my legs aside, astonishing and worrying me with his strength. "This time you'll like what I do to you, white woman. When my cock dances inside of you, you'll scream with pleasure."

I swallowed nervously.

Chapter Eleven

The stars in the heavens bore witness to my seduction, and, as I stared at them, I marveled at what the Indian was doing to me, his face buried between my legs. I had tried to fight him off...I truly had...but...after his tongue slid across my clitoris, I lost the battle. From across the cornfield came the distinct sounds of a woman's moans, and it was Millie. Her Indian had seduced her as well.

Laughing Hawk's skill at cunnilingus wasn't to be underestimated, and, as he speared me, I closed my eyes. "Ooohh...no..." I had never had a man touch me like this before. Their tongues were stronger and longer than females. His thumb grazed my nub, flicking gently, yet persistently, against the inflamed mass. It was shameful to be writhing and trembling at the hands of a bloodthirsty heathen, but my young, lustful body wouldn't obey my mind. "Stop it now," I breathed, sounding less than convincing.

He kissed my inner thighs, leaving a moist path, while he pressed against my clit with his thumb, maintaining the sensual path I was on. I didn't want to feel this good, my body quivering and my tummy fluttering. Sensing the condition I was in, he came between my thighs, his cock extended. The light from the fire flickered off his skin, revealing a lean body rippling with muscles. I felt him at my entrance, hard and demanding, and with one thrust, he was in deep, slapping my pussy with his balls.

"Oh, my!" This felt so much better than when he had taken me before. This time I was prepared for the intrusion; my juices had slickened the tight passage, allowing him to glide effortlessly. This sensation, coupled with his previous attentions, left me panting, my heart racing wildly. I hadn't expected it to feel this good. I didn't want to enjoy it. I should fight him off…I should…but…the tingling in my center began to blaze uncontrollably. From experience, I knew I wouldn't last long. "No!" I gasped. "Ooohhh…God…nooooo…" I shuddered, biting my lip, as wave after wave of sensation swept over me. "Oh, you dirty heathen!" It was marvelous having a penis inside of me. What a revelation! What a magnificent instrument.

He uttered something in a language I didn't understand, thrusting vigorously. Then he stiffened, emptying his seed in measured squirts. His eyes were closed, long black lashes sweeping his cheeks. The expression on his face was an amalgam of pain and rapture. Something moved behind him, a flash of white, and then a loud thump registered. He gasped, and he looked as if he were going to say something, his mouth forming an O. Blood trickled down the side of his neck, but, instead of speaking, he collapsed on top of me. I struggled to breathe. He was heavier than he looked.

"I'm sorry I couldn't come sooner." It was Millie. "I'm sorry he took you, honey. I would've spared you that, but I couldn't."

"Millie, oh, dear God." I struggled to get out from under him.

"Are you hurt?"

"No." The Indian's cock was lodged deep, but the hardness had begun to soften. "Help get him off me!"

She shoved the prone form none too gently. He rolled onto the blanket, blood trickling down the side of his face. "Come on, girl. Let's rescue Isabelle and get the hell outta here!"

"Where are my clothes?"

A white bundle flew my way. "Here."

"Thank you."

"He's got a knife on him. It's in his belt. I'm taking it."

"What about the bows and arrows?"

"Don't know how to use them."

"Is there a rifle?"

"Don't see one."

"What happened to you?"

"He raped me. I bore it. I tricked him into thinking I liked it, and I…er…got the upper hand so to speak. He's unconscious or dead. I don't know or care. They didn't show the people on the train any mercy. Why the hell should I care? I should kill this one."

I panicked. "No. Don't. He'll have a nice goose egg as a reminder. He won't mess with a white woman again." Shame washed over me. She had pretended to enjoy her Indian's attentions, while I…had truly enjoyed Laughing Hawk. *Oh, you're a loose woman, Ms. Collins.* I had heard murmurings about my mother…about the jungle. She had known the natives there. No one had forced her. It humbled me to think that I wasn't any better than her, although I had thought myself to be.

It's a family trait. Your grandfather liked orgies.

Let's not dredge up history that may or may not be accurate.

Fine. But you still enjoyed that Indian.

Oh, be quiet!

"Where's Isabelle?"

"Over there." Millie pointed to the field. "Come on. We haven't got all night."

"I'm a mess." There was sperm running down my

inner thighs. What if I fell pregnant? *Oh, dear God!*

Millie gripped her stick. "We're gonna sneak up on him and whack him. If that don't work, stab him. Got it?"

How awful. I swallowed hard. "I never in my life thought I'd ever—"

"Desperate times call for desperate measures."

"I suppose they do."

"Do you want to stay? I could leave you here."

"No, of course not."

"They killed your fiancé. They killed all those people on the train."

"You don't need to talk me into it, Millie. I'm with you."

"Good."

We wandered through the field, the wild corn towering over us. My bare feet were filthy, and my nightgown was torn in places and splattered with blood, but I would worry about my appearance at another time. We had survived a train wreck and an Indian kidnapping. Now we had to rescue one of our own. The sound of moaning indicated which section of the field Isabelle was in, and, as Millie and I neared, we braced ourselves. I clutched the knife, my hand trembling.

Two bodies appeared between the stalks of corn, illuminated by the glow of the moon. They glistened in their nakedness, covered in perspiration. "Oh, fuck me, you dirty heathen," moaned Isabelle. She sat on her captor, her hips thrusting back and forth, while his hands gripped her hips. Lush, full breasts bounced with the movement of her body. Her head was back, and long strands of dark hair fell all the way to her bottom.

I glanced at Millie, who looked sternly determined.

The sight of Isabelle fornicating willingly didn't seem to surprise her. She held up a heavy-looking stick and indicated silently that we should approach. The Indian was oblivious, ensnared in the rapture of his captive. His eyes were closed, and his mouth was slightly open.

"Oh, my! Oh…fuck me! Fuck me!" Her fingertips dug into his belly, as she moaned. "It's so good!" She shuddered over him, while he uttered something, thrusting vigorously.

Millie advanced stealthily, lifting the stick and bringing it down over his head with a crack. I cringed at her actions, squeezing my eyes shut. A female scream shattered the night. "Millie? Oh, my God!" Isabelle sounded breathless. "D-did you kill him?"

"Who cares? Get your clothes on. We're getting outta here."

Isabelle glanced at me, smiling slightly. Her look revealed shame, surprise, and relief. "We can't go back to the train. It's under attack."

"We'll take the horses and make a run for it. Get his weapon."

"That was a brave thing you did." Admiration shone in her eyes. "You're a tough lady."

Millie ignored the praise. "Are you hurt?"

"N-no…I'm fine."

"We all did what we had to do to survive. God won't judge us for this. I didn't take a life. I might've injured some thick skulls, but they'll live."

Isabelle grinned. "A white woman bested them! That's rich." Her hands were on her hips. "Aren't we a sight? We look like something the cat spat out." Her laughter was infectious, considering the horrors we had suffered, and I couldn't help smiling.

"We'll find a town and clean up," said Millie. "Get

his horse."

"I hope you don't expect me to navigate. I've the worst sense of direction. I get lost in my own house sometimes."

"We should hurry," I said. "They might wake up."

"Exactly," Millie agreed.

We trotted side by side through a never-ending prairie, the grass tickling my legs. I sat astride, heedless of the undignified and unladylike position; I was too exhausted to care. After more than an hour, it was obvious we were lost. Dark clouds had gathered, and the sky flashed with lightning.

"Is that coming our way?" asked Isabelle.

"I hope not." Millie seemed to relish being on the horse; her expression was alert and thoughtful. Strawberry blonde hair hung down her back, nearly touching her thighs. "This sure is pretty country."

"What if we get attacked by Indians again?" I glanced around warily. "This is their territory." We could be ambushed at any second, for all we knew.

"Don't make any noise, and they won't know we're here," said Isabelle.

"If you say so." My arm ached, but at least my forehead had stopped bleeding. I thought about Edmund. "Do you think they killed everyone on the train?"

Millie glanced at me. "Honey, don't fret about it. I'm sure Edmund's fine."

"We should've gone back to the train." Doubt chipped away at me. Had we made a mistake?

"My brother didn't die. I know he didn't." Isabelle gazed straight ahead. "He had a pistol on him. He always carries one."

An uncomfortable silence filled the air, as we

thought about what we might have lost. I felt shame for enjoying the Indian.

You did what you had to do to survive.

I guess…

I would push the memory out of my mind and pretend it hadn't happened.

We were at the edge of a field; our horses had led us into a line of trees. The smell of wet earth filled my senses. "There's water around here."

"The horses want to go this way. They want a drink," said Millie. "I could use one myself. I'm parched."

"You don't think the animals are going home, do you?" Would we end up in an Indian camp?

"Don't worry about that. We're free now. They can't get us."

"That's a lake or something," said Isabelle. She slid from her horse, patting her flank. "You're a good girl." She led her mare towards the water's edge. "Looks big."

It was a long way down without help. "Ouch." I stepped on something sharp.

"I'll take her," said Millie, reaching for my rope. "Go wash up. Have a drink."

"Thank you." My modesty seemed to have vanished, as I brought the nightgown over my head and left it on the ground. I desperately wanted to remove the smell of the Laughing Hawk from my person. "Omigosh, it's cold." I waded into the lake, my feet encountering a soggy bottom. The humidity had kept me in a state of constant perspiration, and it was a relief to be able to wash off. I dunked under, wetting my hair completely.

"I'm doing that," said Isabelle. "I've never been so dirty in my life." My future sister-in-law joined me, scrubbing her face vigorously. "It's cold but wonderful."

Millie waded out to us. "This just proves Murphy's Law."

"What's that?" I asked.

"Oh, it's a saying. If anything can go wrong, it usually does, at the worst possible time. The story of my life."

"You're always so optimistic," I giggled.

"It's my unshakable sense of tragedy that gets me through the short periods of joy," she laughed. "It's the way of the Irish."

"But what an adventure!" exclaimed Isabelle. "The things we'll tell our grandchildren. How many people have survived a train wreck? How many have survived an Indian attack?"

"We're stuck in the middle of nowhere," I grumbled. "We may not survive at all."

"We'll do just fine," said Millie. "A town's around here somewhere."

"When my father hears of the accident, he'll send help."

"What about tonight? Where will we sleep?"

"We need to find shelter," said Millie. "Let's get dressed and go. That storm sounds like it's getting closer."

I trudged from the lake, ringing out my hair. "Gosh, I'm freezing." I snatched the nightgown off the ground.

"How's your arm?" asked Millie.

"It's sore, but I'll live." I tossed the garment over my head, thrusting my hands through the armholes. The wetness of my hair dampened the material instantly. "There has to be something out here."

Isabelle groaned. "I don't know about that."

Millie flung her hair over her shoulder, grabbing her mare's mane. "Now I gotta get on this thing. Stirrups would be helpful."

"I'll lift you, Sarah," said Isabelle. "You're shorter than me."

"Thank you." She threaded her hands together, and I used them as a step. "There is something about riding bareback. It's freeing."

"Call it freeing all you want, but it hurts my ass," grumbled Isabelle.

"We'll all be sore tomorrow," said Millie. "No doubt about that."

We set out under ominous skies, the wind had picked up, and thunder rumbled threateningly. We hadn't been riding for more than thirty minutes, when lights flickered in the distance.

"There's something up ahead!" shouted Millie, as a clap of thunder resounded. "Head towards it!" She sat forward, loosening the grip on the reins, and gave three quick kicks into the horse's side, spurring the mare into a gallop. "Heeaw! Come on girls!"

Chapter Twelve

Isabelle and I followed, racing across an expanse of savanna that stretched on towards the horizon. Droplets of rain lashed my face, as incandescent veins of lightning flashed across the sky. The lights in question belonged to a small house, situated against a backdrop of trees, whose limbs blew in the approaching storm. Several horses were in a small coral. They neighed and snorted at our approach.

I glanced warily at Millie. "I don't know about this." Unease pricked me. Who was in the house, Indians, bandits, or worse?

The sound of male laughter drifted to us from an open window.

Millie dismounted and unsheathed her knife. She looked fierce and wild, with windswept hair and torn clothing. "I'm not afraid of a couple of men." She had proven herself to be formidable where they were concerned.

Isabelle tied her horse to a fence. "Let's get this over with. I'm tired. I'll sleep on the floor if I have to."

I glanced warily at the house. "Are you sure about this? We could find a field to sleep in."

"Don't worry, honey. I won't let anything happen to you. Come on down from that horse—"

The front door flew open, and Millie found herself staring down the barrel of a rifle. The owner of the weapon was dressed in trousers and a crumpled shirt; the sleeves were folded up on each arm. His expression was hidden beneath a wide-brim hat. "And what do we have here?" The timber in his voice was deep and melodic.

I sat atop my horse; the thought to flee swept through me like wildfire, but there was something familiar about the stranger.

"We're women seeking shelter, sir!" yelled Millie. "We've survived an Indian attack…and a train wreck. Put your gun down."

"Put your knife down." There were two men behind him, holding weapons. "You sneak up on my house, and you think I won't protect myself?"

"We need help, sir," said Isabelle. "We've been through quite an ordeal. It would be kindly of you to let us in and offer us food and a bed. There's a storm coming."

"Kindly, huh?" he laughed. "You ladies want to share our bed, eh? I got nothin' against that sort of thing. My boys and I would be mighty obliged to have you fine ladies as our…guests."

"Ouf! These men are scoundrels, Millie! I knew this was a bad idea."

The stranger tipped his hat, eyeing me. "Well, I'll be damned. You're that woman from the train."

I gasped, recognizing the blackguard. "You're the bandit who stole my engagement ring!"

"Still sore about that, huh?" He lowered the rifle. "You say you were attacked by Indians?"

"They sabotaged the tracks and wrecked the train," said Isabelle. "We were on our way to Omaha."

"Dang, that'll be big news."

"Might make us look like small potatoes," said the man behind him.

"Oh, the law will still be lookin' for us. Don't doubt that, Buck."

"Are we gonna let these pretty women inside?" asked a thin, blond haired man. "They look like they need help. We'd sure be happy to help them. I know I would."

"Don't think for one second that any of you will be laying one hand on me," asserted Millie. "You won't be touching my ward either."

Brack's eyes roamed over me, pausing on my breasts. "That's a shame." It was clear what he wanted to do to me, and, remembering his kiss, my body began humming with arousal. "Let me get you down from that horse, honey." He handed his rifle to Buck. Without waiting for a reply, he pulled me down and straight into his arms. A muscled arm snaked around my back, drawing me close.

"Stop that!" I struggled against him.

"It's like Christmas and birthday all wrapped up in one sexy package." There was a hint of alcohol on his breath. "Happy Birthday to me."

"You let her go!" demanded Millie. "Get your hands off her."

"I don't think she minds all that much." His eyes had yet to leave my face. I blinked at him stupidly.

"Sarah!" barked Millie. "Wake up, girl!"

"Um…" I pushed against him, feeling nothing but muscle. "Don't."

Isabelle rolled her eyes. "That'll scare him off. Oh, fuck it!" For a lady, Isabelle's use of language was shocking. "I'm tired. I don't care if they're bandits." She slid from the horse. "I wouldn't mind some whiskey, boys. Please tell me you have some left."

"Now there's a woman after my own heart," murmured the blond man. His grin went from ear to ear, exposing a mouth full of chipped and missing teeth. "Come on in. Make yourselves at home. I'll pour you a drink."

"Well, that's kind of you."

Brack had yet to let go of me, and I had yet to object, although I should. His hand drifted to my buttocks, where he grasped my soft flesh, squeezing it gently.

"Oh!" I gasped, as a rush of tingles raced through me.

Millie hit him. "That's enough now!" She smacked the side of his head.

He covered his face. "Hey!"

She grabbed my hand. "Get inside. It's about to rain."

The house wasn't bigger than a shack and almost as rustic. There were shelves built into the walls and one small, lumpy bed. There were bedrolls on the floor and several bottles of whiskey. A large satchel brimmed with hidden goodies, and I suspected these were the items stolen from train robberies.

Isabelle downed her drink. "Oh, that's good. Pour some more in there, cowboy."

"Yes, ma'am."

"What's your name?"

"Jimmy."

"What's a fine young man such as yourself doing robbing trains?"

"Well, Miss, my family didn't have much. My pa died when I was five, and my ma drank herself to death. I fell in with the wrong crowd," he eyed Brack, "and the rest is history."

I sat on a rickety chair, just as an enormous boom sounded overhead and the heavens opened up, lashing rain down upon us. Brack hung his hat on a peg and sat next to me. He stared with such intensity that the hair stood up on my arms.

"Here you go," said Jimmy. "Have a drink."

"Thank you." I took a sip, the liquid burning a path down my throat.

"I don't want booze," muttered Milly. "Drink is the curse of the land."

"That's right," laughed Brack. "You Irish could'a ruled the world, if you hadn't invented whiskey."

Millie glared at him. "You better watch out for that one. He'll steal the sugar outta your punch, if you let him."

"So I assume we're with the infamous Corbett Gang?" asked Isabelle. "Add that to the list of things I can tell my grandchildren about."

Exhaustion seeped into my weary bones, producing a lengthy yawn. I seemed to have Brack's undivided attention, although I wasn't speaking.

"We might need to turn the lights down, boys. The ladies are tired."

"Sarah and Isabelle will take the bed," stated Millie. "I'll sleep on the floor."

"I don't think so." Those warm eyes were on me. "You sleep on the bed with Isabelle. Sarah's with me."

Millie bristled. "I think not, sir!"

Oh, my goodness! That look all but singed my nerve endings, stealing my will to argue. For some reason, I could not resist this man, and that didn't seem to bother me at all.

"My bedroll is mighty comfy." His grin brought out the lines around his eyes. "I've never had any complaints before."

A smile stole across my face. "You take the bed, Millie. I'm fine. I won't let him touch me."

Her stare burned holes in my back. "You've lost your senses. He's a villain of the worst sort, and you're going to sleep with him?"

"We're all in the same room. Nothing's going to happen." I muttered, "I'm too tired."

Brack brought his hand down on the table, rattling the whisky bottle. "It's settled then. Let's make ourselves a little more comfortable, shall we?" His grin was hot sex personified, mixed with a dangerous, raw quality that appealed to me on nearly every level. "I'll get the bedroll out."

I was nearly dizzy with exhaustion, and the whisky had relaxed my inhibitions. "Do you have a pillow?" My voice was breathy soft and barely above a whisper.

"Honey, that's what my arm's for."

Millie snorted. "How I'm going to explain this to your mother, I'll never know." She lifted the covers on the bed. "If there are bugs in here, I'll scream."

"That bed's fine. No bedbugs. Honest," said Jimmy. "Slept in it last night, and I've got no bites on me anywhere." He grasped his crotch. "Although this is larger than it should be. Anybody wanna help me out?" Brack and Buck snorted with laughter.

"Ha!" said Isabelle. "You boys might be gun slinging train robbers, but that doesn't mean you have any skill whatsoever below the waist."

"Whoa...that sounds like a challenge, boys," said Brack. "Your virility is being called into question. You gonna stand for that?"

Jimmy undid his belt. "That's fine. I'll be happy to prove her wrong. I bet she's never been with a real man before. I'll show her what for."

"You're welcome to try, train robber." She got on the bed, grinning. "This little disaster might not be such a bad time after all."

"Shush now," admonished Millie. "Don't encourage

them."

"Come here." Brack held out a hand.

"My back will ache tomorrow."

"What happened to your arm? It's all blue."

"Train crash. I landed on it."

"You got lucky, honey. I bet a lotta folks died."

Images of smoke, charred bodies, and blood filled my vision. "They did." I scooted closer, and he grabbed me, dragging me to him. "It was horrible."

He sighed. "You go to sleep. It'll all look better in the morning."

"I hope so."

"Merry Christmas to me," he murmured.

He smelled of leather, horse, whiskey, and perspiration. He was all man and then some. The arms around me felt strong. He vibrated with masculine energy, heady and seductive. I closed my eyes, blotting out the horrors of the night, and fell into a deep, dreamless sleep.

Chapter Thirteen

I wasn't even going to pretend to be asleep, as the touch of a man's hand skimmed over my hip. At some point during the night, I had turned from him, and the bottom portion of my nightgown had worked its way up my thigh. He'd divested himself of clothing; his shirt was off, and his pants were missing. Not one word of complaint came from my lips regarding this change in circumstance. Fingers skimmed over my thigh to my hip and back again, leaving a path of little flutters that had me clamping my lips together, preventing a moan from escaping.

"Good morning, sweetheart," he whispered, huskily.

"Don't touch me."

His soft laughter teased my ear. "You and me both want it. Don't even try to pretend."

I opened an eye to take a peek around the room. Isabelle and Millie were fast asleep, and the other bandits were unconscious on the floor. Feeling slightly less conspicuous now, I wiggled closer to Brack. He responded by kissing my neck, which sent shivers down my spine.

"Ooohh…"

"Sheee…honey…"

His roaming hand had slid between my thighs, a finger rubbing my heated core. The fact that he slid inside easily gave away the extent of my desire, highlighting my arousal, and all but giving him permission to do as he pleased. A finger opened me, and a second finger filled me, working in deeper.

"Kiss me," he murmured.

I turned to glance at him, noting a sleepy looking man with bleary eyes and messy hair. I'd never seen anything sexier in my whole life, and as his fingers drove through the silken confines of my pussy, my lips met his. The memory of the kiss on the train came crashing through my consciousness, hot, quick, and demanding. His lips were soft, yet persistent; his tongue devouring me and mine invading his. I held nothing back in that heated instant, enjoying the taste and feel of him.

His thumb grazed my nub, triggering a flood of pleasure that fanned out to every part of my body. I felt wetness on my thighs, which should have embarrassed me; instead, I wiggled closer to him, hoping he would enter me. Answering the silent request, he prodded me with a thick shaft, the tip rounded and broad. A little push and he was buried, producing a slight stinging sensation. I was sore from when Laughing Hawk had taken my virginity.

"Honey," he breathed. "It's so tight."

"If my mother knew I was letting a filthy train robber touch me, she would disown me."

His laughter filled my ears. "You ain't exactly fighting me, darlin'."

"I should…"

Soft lips kissed the skin on my throat, his teeth nipping gently. "Why fight? It's what we both want. I knew it the first time I saw you. That's why I kissed you. If I didn't take what I wanted, it would be gone. I didn't think I'd ever see you again. Now what I don't understand is how fate brought you to my doorstep. That's got me puzzled as hell."

"I don't know either…ooohh…don't stop."

He grasped my hip, thrusting deeper. "Like that?"

His voice was low and rich.

"Yes." My hand slid to my pussy, where I rubbed myself, producing a distracting tingling. "A little more."

"Does this fiancé of yours know you ain't a virgin?"

"Shush!"

"You be sure to tell him that a good for nothin' gunslinger had his cock in you. You tell him how you screamed when I fucke—"

"Oh! You...horrible...man...ooohhhh..." I wasn't able to say anything else because the orgasm stole the breath from my lungs. I shuddered, thrashing against him, my pussy contracting sharply.

"Good Lord," he murmured. "You're a hot one."

My forehead was on my arm. "Oh, shut up."

He continued to drive deep, pounding me soundly. Then he pulled free. "Wrap your lips around me," he rasped.

That suggestion was wickedness personified, but...being utterly curious about what his instrument looked like and never having seen one before up close and personal, my inquisitiveness won out by a mile, leaving my morals and my sense of decency on the front doorstep. I wrapped a hand around him, feeling hot, sticky wetness.

"What do I do?"

"Don't bite...at least not hard. Suck on it."

I had caught a glimpse of the Indian's cock, and it looked as if skin covered it, like a snug blanket. This one was free of skin, surprisingly long, and wondrously hard. I smelled myself on him, which reminded me of having sex with Millie. As streams of sunlight filtered in through the cracks in the walls, I set about licking the tip of a magnificent looking penis. The bandit fell onto his back, closing his eyes. I laved attention to the leaking tip, wiping away clear fluid with my tongue.

"Oh, honey."

"Am I doing this right?" I whispered.

"Yes…"

"Okay."

He grasped his balls, pulling them away from his body. "Lick these too."

The soft looking sacs were coated in sparse wisps of hair. A musky aroma teased my nose. I sucked a ball and prodded it with my tongue, feeling the heat of him and wondering how good something like this would feel, if I were a man. The same amount of attention was bestowed upon its mate. When both had been thoroughly attended to, I ran my tongue up the length of his shaft, while he fingered his crown.

"Ooohh…honey…Oh! Shit!"

I was going to suck him again, but the tip suddenly erupted in a spritz of whitish fluid. "Oh, my."

"Oh my's right," quipped Jimmy, who eyed us from across the room. "I wouldn't mind being woken up like that."

I buried my face in Brack's chest out of embarrassment. "Ugh."

"There are other women," he chuckled. "This one's mine."

"Those bitches ain't nearly as friendly."

"How do you know?" Isabelle sat up. Her hair was a riot of tangles around her shoulders. "Maybe if you were better at seduction like Mr. Corbett here, you might find women more receptive."

"Christ! These women are smart. I don't even understand half of them words."

Brack held me close. "Merry Christmas to me."

"Stop saying that," I giggled. "I'm not a present."

"Oh, yes you are. You're the answer to my prayers. Too bad I won't live long enough to enjoy it."

"What do you mean?"

"I'm headin' for a hangin', honey. A nice, tight noose is in my future. Sooner than later. Maybe today."

"No."

"Yes. Make no mistake about it. I'm livin' on borrowed time. That being said, I'm gonna speak my mind. You're the prettiest thing I've ever seen, and I could love you so easy. I could marry you and have babies with you. I could grow old with you." He gazed at me. "I'm seein' us on rocking chairs, sipping ice tea with grandbabies all around." He moved a strand of hair away from my face. "Thank you for a lifetime of happiness."

I swallowed the lump in my throat. "Oh, Brack." The immediacy of the situation hit home like a perfectly aimed rock. The meanings of his words were bittersweet, tinged with the tragic undertones of impending doom. These few hours together would be the only ones we had.

"I need to use the facilities," muttered Millie. Her unhappy glare was directed towards me. "Don't think I didn't hear everything."

"I'm sorry." I turned, staring at her. "I wanted to resist him. I...really did."

She snorted in reply, flinging a shapely leg over the side of the bed. "Try not to get into trouble while I'm gone." She glared at me. "I wasn't speaking to you. You've already gone and done it."

"He's gonna hang soon, Millie, and he's...adorable." I glanced at Brack. "What a shame."

"The sooner we get to California, the better." She padded to the door. "Which way to the privy?"

"Open your lungs, and take a whiff," said Jimmy. "You can't miss it."

"Thanks."

"So, Jimmy," said Isabelle. "What do you have to offer a girl?" She had woken up on the saucy side of the street this morning.

He stood, dropping his pants, and exposing an impressive looking cock. "This here is eight inches of prime cut meat, Miss Isabelle. It's all yours for the very low price of a wink and a smile."

Isabelle scratched her chin. "Hum…how many ladies have had the pleasure of this…eight inch blessing?"

"Not that many. It's hard to get…er…pleasure on the run. It's not everyday the Lord sends us three beautiful women dressed in nothin' but night clothes."

"Indeed." Her smile was sassy, as she lifted the garment over her head, tossing it to the floor. "Why don't you bring that blessing over here and let me get a better look at it."

"Yes, ma'am!"

Chapter Fourteen

Brack's chuckling was contagious. My soon to be sister-in-law was playing the part of the floosy, but one had to wonder how much of her behavior was acting and how much of it was the real Isabelle.

"You're an impressive stud, big boy." She wrapped her hand around his cock. "Oh, the games we could play."

"Ahem. It's hardly fair to leave me out now, is it?" asked Buck. "I've got my own God given gifts, and I wouldn't mind lending a hand. Looks like that's a lotta woman for one man."

"Is that so?" Isabelle stroked Jimmy's cock, the object appearing even larger than before. "What exactly do you bring to the table?"

Buck was on his feet in a flash. "Nine inches, ma'am. Why mess with the boy, when you can have the man."

"Nine inches? My goodness."

"Hard and ready, ma'am."

Brack pulled me to him, whispering, "I've been praying for a miracle, Ms. Collins. God was listening for once."

I stared into his eyes; flecks of grey tinged the irises to smoky brown. "I can't get involved with a criminal," I whispered, mostly to myself.

"I think I need to have a better look, Buck," said Isabelle. "You're so far away."

His tall, lanky form bounded towards the bed. "Is this close enough?"

"I do believe it is." Her hand closed around the twitching shaft. "Nine inches, huh? Isn't that…stretching the truth a little?"

"No, ma'am, it isn't. You're more than welcome to keep touching it, Miss Isabelle. That feels really nice."

The door opened, bringing a gust of hot air. "What in the Dickens is happening here?" Millie's hands rested on her hips. "Have you all taken leave of your senses?"

"What fine looking cocks," said Isabelle. "These gentlemen are on the run. They're going to be hung soon. What's the harm in a little…fun?" She glanced at Brack. "Have you killed anyone?"

"I haven't, but Buck has."

This seemed to please her. "They're thieves and murderers. They'll be captured soon. They won't be around for much longer. It would be the Christian…ah…the charitable thing to give them something to remember us by." She gasped, "Oohh…you boys are getting harder by the second. You could probably hammer a spike through a trestle with one of these."

Jimmy grinned. "Yes, ma'am. I do believe I could."

Millie let out a long sigh. "Isabelle, if I didn't know you as a lady of excellent breeding and character, I'd seriously be questioning things right now."

"That's not fair, Millie," I said. "I heard you in the cornfield last night with that Indian. You might've been waiting for the opportunity to hit him in the head, but you enjoyed yourself while you were waiting."

"I think we all enjoyed those Indians last night," said Isabelle. "Let's quit pretending. Whatever is said and done here will follow these men to the grave. Our reputations are quite safe." She squeezed the end of Jimmy's cock, producing a fat drop of pre-cum. "I hope you don't mind, but I'm having a taste." She wrapped her lips around him, sucking noisily.

"You're more than welcome to a helping of Buck," offered the outlaw, who spoke to Millie. "I've a fondness for redheads."

"Do you now?"

"Yes, ma'am."

"You remind me of my husband."

"That's a mighty kind thing of you to say."

"Not really. He was a cheat and a scoundrel and a drunkard. The happiest day of my life was when he died."

I gasped. I had never heard her speak so ill of her husband. "Millie!"

She held up a hand. "Since we're being honest and since none of this will ever be spoken of outside this shack, I'll say that I prefer to have sex with women. I never did feel lust for a man. I'll join you scoundrels and that brazen hussy," she pointed at Isabelle, "but don't think I'll enjoy it. Not for one second."

"Oh, Millie," I laughed. "You're in rare form this morning."

She harrumphed, and sat on the bed, while Isabelle sucked vigorously on Jimmy's cock. She spread her legs, exposing a pink slit, surrounded by dark blonde hair. "Who wants a taste of Ireland?"

"Well, Goddamn, but I will," said Buck. "I don't care if you're a lesbian. I get my pussy any way I can."

"That feels so nice," groaned Jimmy. "I wanna fuck you, Miss Isabelle. I'd be obliged, if you could bend over the table."

She grinned saucily. "Well, there's an idea." She slid from the bed and leaned over the piece of furniture, her rounded bottom in the air. "I'm ready, Jimmy."

"Hot damn!" He was on her in a flash, prodding her with a rigid cock. "Oh, thank you…"

"Jimmy!" she gasped. "You filthy bandit."

"Yes, ma'am."

I glanced at Brack. His expression was wistful, yet slightly sad. "What's wrong?"

"Nothin' a kiss won't fix."

I wrapped my arms around his neck, holding him close. "Like this?" I touched his lips, tasting him.

"Yes, honey. Just like that."

"Oh, Lord, that's a talented tongue," murmured Millie. "You keep that up, Buck. Don't…stop…"

Isabelle was pounded against the table, the wood creaking under the assault. "Oh-you-dirty-boys!" Jimmy's cock plunged with each punishing thrust. "You sure are well-equipped! You weren't joking about that."

"This here is a mighty fine pussy," said Jimmy. "Nice and tight."

"Ooohh…thanks…" she groaned. "Don't stop, you dirty train robber."

I sat on Brack's lap, feeling his cock prodding my bottom. His hands grasped my waist, the palms running up the sides of my body to cup my breasts. His teeth grazed my neck, sending pinpricks of pleasure through me, which centered in my lower anatomy.

"Oh, fuck me, you dirty outlaw!"

"You rich, white bitch!"

"Ooohh…God…I…can't stand it!" Isabelle shuddered, dropping her face to the table. "Ooohhh…that was so good."

"I'm still rarin' to go. I'm harder than oak."

"You sure are." She sounded breathless. "You worked me good."

"Give it a suck, honey." Isabelle dropped to her knees, taking him in her mouth. "Yeah, that's it."

"Let's move like this," whispered Brack. In the next

instant, I straddled him, and he was in me. "There. That's better." His cock felt enormous in my tight tunnel. "Tell me how much you like me."

"I don't even know you."

"Lie to me. Pretend you know me. Pretend I'm your fiancé."

"Oh, Brack."

"We don't have alotta time, darlin'. Tell me what you want. Tell me I'm the one you want."

"This is going to sound awful, but you remind me of my dad."

A bark of laughter filled the room. "Now I'm really worried."

"I didn't mean it like that! I mean…the way you say darlin' and your manner. I can tell you're a good man. I don't know how you got yourself involved with robbing trains, but you're not a bad man."

"After my crops failed and my wife died, I had no choice. I got two kids, and they need food, Sarah."

"You have children?"

"They're with my sister. I send money to support them, but…shit! I've made alotta mistakes. Too many. I can't turn back now."

"How old are your kids?"

"Jessie's five, and Melanie's four."

"You have a little girl?"

"Yes, I do." A flash of pain glimmered in his eyes, and then it was gone. "I've let 'em down. I've dishonored our name." His head dropped. "Now's not the time to talk about this."

"You wanted us to get to know each other."

"Pretend you love me," he whispered fiercely. "Lie to me. Tell me you love me."

"Oh, Brack." His earnest expression softened my

heart. "Something like that might not be a lie." I shouldn't feel so emotional about a stranger. "I do love you."

"Now that's what I want to hear." He kissed me, sliding his tongue past my lips, seducing me thoroughly.

"It's a shame."

"What is?"

"That I'm engaged and you'll be hanged."

"It is."

My nub rubbed against his pelvis, creating a buzz that produced delightful tremors. I had all the control in this position, and I found that I enjoyed working him at my own pace. It wouldn't be long before I let it all go and gave in to the orgasm that inched its way closer by the second.

"That's it, suck me," moaned Jimmy. "Oohhh…yeah. Open up, you pretty thing." Isabelle waited beneath him with her tongue out, while he massaged his rounded tip. "Oohh…Jesus…ooohh…" A stream of white spunk jetted, catching her forehead and splattering over her tongue.

Millie moaned, flinging her head against the bed. Buck had satisfied the fiery redhead, bringing her to completion with a lengthy and talented tongue. The scene in the shack was wildly erotic and so debauched, I almost didn't believe it was happening.

My hips thrust harder. "That's it. You're gettin' it. Work me, honey," groaned Brack. "Use me."

"Are you gonna suck my dick or what?" asked Buck.

"I guess, if I have to," muttered Millie.

"There's the spirit."

"Don't expect me to swallow it."

"Just suck me, you Irish bitch."

"Oh, Brack." My fingertips dug into his shoulders, while I rode him, feeling him deep. The heat in the small dwelling had become oppressive, leaving a thin sheen of perspiration on my body. It smelled like sex, potent and musky.

"That's it. Work me."

I kissed him, our tongues battling sensuously. His arms went around me, holding me close, our slick skin rubbing, straining for release. I moaned, and shuddered from the pleasure that rocked my system. "Oh, my Lord!" I trembled and convulsed with each contraction, my pussy compressing his cock. "Oooohhh...Brack..."

"Oh, Jesus." He thrust up into me, stiffening. "Ooohhh...Sarah..." We clung together, our mouths fused, as we rode out the tiny, blissful aftershocks. "It was so good, honey."

"It was." I sounded exhausted.

Buck groaned, spraying cream into Millie's face. "Yeah! Now you're getting it."

"Ugh. That's disgusting."

He chuckled in reply.

Chapter Fifteen

Breakfast was stale bread and dried jerky, but I didn't mind. Brack and I wandered down to the lake for a swim. Afterwards, we sat in the grass, and I appreciated the way the sun hit the water, producing thousands of brilliant flashes. I was cradled between his legs, leaning against him.

"How long have you been robbing trains?"

"About a year."

"What did you do with my engagement ring?"

"Nothing yet. I got a jeweler who melts the gold down and sells the stones. He's in Pennsylvania. I haven't been able to see him."

"That ring was in Edmund's family for a hundred years."

"Sorry about that. I still have it, if you want it."

"No. Never mind."

"Are you in love with him?"

"I thought so."

"What about now?"

"He might be dead for all I know. The Indians attacked the train after they derailed it. He...could have passed away."

"I'm sorry you had to go through that."

I turned to stare at him. "You're sorry? You robbed my train! You pointed weapons in people's faces and stole their possessions. Now you say you're sorry?"

He shrugged, looking sheepish. "It's my job. Some people work in banks or in offices. I just happen to be a robber by profession. Scaring the tar outta innocent people is a part of the job." He grinned crookedly. "Sorry."

"That's a horrible justification."

"It is, but it's the only one I got."

"Can't you do something else with yourself? Can't you study a trade or work for a legitimate business?"

"Robbing is lucrative. I was a lousy farmer."

"It's dangerous."

"It is."

"Then stop it."

"It's too late. I made a bad decision a year ago. Buck asked for help. He and Jimmy had the idea that robbing one train would set us up for life. We had our guns out before we even boarded, and the passengers hid their valuables. We only got about three hundred dollars and some watches that weren't worth nothin'. We had to rob another train to make up for it, and, by that time, it was too late. I was a wanted man."

"Now you can't walk away."

"No ma'am. They'd find me. I could run for a while, but it would delay the inevitable. My kind don't fare so well in the courts, and with good reason."

"What if you had a lawyer?"

"Can't afford one."

I had a trust from my grandmother. "I could get you one."

"Don't bother. It wouldn't do any good."

"You're awfully pessimistic."

"No, realistic. The odds are stacked against me. I have no one to blame but myself."

The fact that he had given up bothered me. "But don't you want something better for your kids? Shouldn't you be fighting for them? Maybe you could leave the country? Start over somewhere new."

"They're in Missouri with my sister. She's taking care of 'em. It's all I can ask for."

Anger pricked me. "You son of a bitch! Those kids deserve to have their dad. If you were to ask them, they'd say all they want is you."

"Then what do you recken I do?"

"Let me hire a lawyer. He'll get you off with as little prison time as possible, and you can start over."

"With you?"

"I-I don't know." That question had surprised me.

"So you ain't a part of the package, huh?"

"I don't know about Edmund. I…he might be alive."

"If he's dead?" A thick, dark brow lifted.

"Then I suppose…"

"Suppose what?"

"I might go with you."

"You'd marry a train robber? You'd raise an outlaw's kids?"

This had to be the craziest notion I had ever entertained. I couldn't believe the words that came out of my mouth. "Yes."

"I think you bumped your head pretty good in the crash." He grinned.

"My mother's going to have kittens." I couldn't possibly break my engagement to Edmund to marry a convicted felon, could I?

He moved hair out of my face. "Honey, I appreciate your concern, but my messes…my disasters are my problem. Be grateful for that. You don't have to fix me."

"Somebody should. You're incapable of helping yourself."

His thumb moved over my lower lip. "You're the most beautiful thing I've ever seen. I'm glad I robbed you. You were my favorite job."

"You make it sound like it's over."

"Sweetheart, it never began." Tears stung my eyes. "Don't do that. I hate it when women cry."

I wrapped my arms around his neck. "Let's stay here for as long as we can."

"We'll run outta food. Our provisions were low to begin with. Your family's worried sick about you. I'm sending you to town. It's due east."

"I'm not going anywhere."

He sighed, his arms tightening around me. "I've no right to fuck up your life like I did mine. I won't let that happen."

I wanted to argue, but I swallowed my disappointment instead, burying my face in his neck. We sat out by the lake and talked for hours, until the sun began to dip behind the trees. The need for food eventually brought us back to the shack. He held my hand, his thumb rubbing my palm, as we walked towards the dilapidated building. The time we had spent together had been easy and relaxing. Nothing about our conversation was forced, and neither of us had to hide our feelings or pretend to feel more than we did. The sun had set, the sky tinged in orange and red streaks. We neared the door.

He drew me into his arms. "I can't wait to make love to you tonight."

"Me either."

"If I wasn't starving, I'd take you right here."

"That's barbaric," I giggled.

"Yeah? I've got a bit of Viking in me. It's on my father's side."

"I'm not surprised."

He held open the door. "After you."

"Thank you."

I was surprised by how dark the interior was. It didn't seem as if anyone was there. "Millie?"

Brack was a step behind me. Something moved out of the corner of my eye, and a thunk sounded. I spun around, shocked. My lover had collapsed to the floor, the result of a rifle striking his head. The man who had hit him glared at me.

"I'm Deputy Sheriff Blain. Are you all right, ma'am?"

Men stepped from the shadows, dressed in uniforms, and they grabbed Brack, lifting his unconscious form off the floor and dragging him from the house.

Alarm raced through me. "What are you doing?"

"Apprehending a wanted man, Miss." His eyes roamed over me, missing nothing. I wore a torn and soiled nightgown and little else.

"Where are you taking him?"

"The county lockup."

"Where are my friends?"

"At a hotel in town. I'll escort you to them."

Bile rose in my throat. "Thank you." I had to send a telegram. He needed a lawyer.

"You're one of the survivors of the train wreck. Your parents and Senator Lakewood will be relieved that you're no longer a hostage."

"T-thank you."

"You've had quite an ordeal. You're a lucky lady."

"Do you know anything about Senator Lakewood's son, Edmund? He was on the train. Is he alive?"

"Yes, ma'am he is. Walked away without a scrape."

I hated the fact that this bit of news disappointed me. "Thank you."

"My men will escort you to town. Someone needs

to look at your forehead. You might need stiches."

"Yes, Sheriff Blain."

Millie and Isabelle were waiting for me in a tidy room on the second floor of the Bromly Hotel. The doctor had treated me in the manager's office, and I had required two stiches. I burst through the door, ready to let the tears that threatened for the last hour overwhelm me.

"There she is!" exclaimed Millie. "Thank the saints!" I collapsed on the bed, the springs creaking, and began to cry. Millie sat next to me; her hand touched my back. "What's the matter, honey? Why are you crying?"

"What happened?" I sobbed. "We walked into an ambush."

"The lawmen were clever," said Isabelle. "Jimmy went out to use the facilities, and he didn't return. Then Buck went after him, and the same thing happened. They were waiting for them. Then they knocked on the door and took us to town. We didn't tell them you were at the lake."

"The house must've been watched," said Millie.

"They have Brack. They took him into custody."

"I'm sorry, honey. I know you were growing fond of the scoundrel."

"They'll hang him!"

Millie sighed. "He's a thieving train robber. I imagine they will."

"Are you hungry?" Isabelle sat on the bed. "We can have food brought up."

An idea suddenly hit me. I sat up, wiping the tears away with the back of my hand. I noticed the trunks on the floor, although they looked damaged. "Is that our luggage?"

"Yes. Thank goodness." Isabelle smiled kindly. "You can change into some—"

"Good." Determination had a steely grip on me. "I need to wash up. Help me with my hair?" I glanced at Millie.

She looked confused. "I...suppose so."

"I need you to do something for me, Isabelle."

"What's that?"

"I need a revolver."

Her mouth fell open. "Oh, dear."

Chapter Sixteen

I sashayed into the jail wearing a cream-colored jacket over a full skirt with draped fabric and an enormous bow at the back. A black hat with fake pink flowers sat askew on top of my head.

"I'm here to see the prisoner."

The man in spectacles behind the counter glanced up, clearly astonished to see me. Wanted posters graced the wall, and I recognized a poorly done drawing of Brack Corbett, which hardly did him justice. He was far more handsome in person.

"Which prisoner, Miss?"

"Brack Corbett."

"Is that so?"

"Yes, sir."

"What would a pretty lady want with a no good train robber?"

"It's personal, Mr...?"

"McCormick."

"It's none of your business, Mr. McCormick."

He scrunched up his face, which made him look peculiar. "Fine. I'll take you back, but I gotta search you first. The last time a woman visited a prisoner she brought in a gun. Can you imagine that?"

"That's shocking."

"The man she gave it to used it on my deputy. Shot him in the arm, and then he got away. It made us all look bad. Real bad. It was another six months before we caught up with him." He smiled, revealing stained teeth. "My deputies shot him to death. Getting even sure is satisfying."

I smiled, but it didn't reach my eyes. "I'm sure it is."

"So, if you'll step over here real quick, I can search you."

"I can hardly wait." Nervous bundles of energy sent my heart racing.

He patted me down, lifting my skirts, searching for a weapon. His hands brushed against my thighs and over my bottom. Several deputies came and went, casting interested looks our way.

One of them muttered, "Don't know why outlaws always get the best lookin' girls."

When he was satisfied that I hadn't concealed a weapon, he led me down a narrow hallway, opening a door, which revealed a dingy looking room filled with metal bars, spanning floor to ceiling.

"Here we are."

I recognized the three men sitting in separate cells. "Well, look who came to visit," said Jimmy. Brack stared at me; his look was vague.

"You got ten minutes." He pointed at Brack. "No funny business, you hear?"

"No, sir," he drawled. "Wouldn't think of it."

"I'll be checking on you."

"I'd be disappointed if you didn't."

"Smart ass," he muttered.

I wrapped my hands around the bars. "Brack."

"What are you doing here?"

I glanced over my shoulder. We were alone. With deliberate hast, I unpinned my hat. The item hidden underneath had given me a cracking headache. I handed him the revolver. "I brought you a present."

"Jesus fucking Christ!"

"This is for you too." I gave him a thick roll of twenty-dollar bills. "And, this." A small piece of paper appeared. "This is my address in Sacramento. I want you to escape and find me. Do you think you can do that?"

His grin was enormous. "You're somethin'."

"Somebody's gotta rescue you."

"Honey…I don't wanna burst your bubble, but…" His look was wistful. "They'll catch up with me sooner or later. This'll only bide us a little time."

"Fine. I don't care." I glanced at Jimmy and Buck. "You boys look comfortable."

"You're an angel, Ms. Collins."

"You got another chance. What you do with it is up to you." My eyes met Brack's. "And you. I'll never forgive you, if you don't find me."

"This is foolish."

I pointed a finger in his face. "I've risked everything for you, you filthy train robber."

His hand thrust through the bars, grabbing me. I was pressed against cold metal. His hot, sultry breath fanned my face. "I'll find you all right. You got a deal, honey."

"That's what I want to hear." I kissed him, his tongue sliding into my mouth. "Oh, Brack…"

He pushed me. "Now get the hell outta here! Get outta town. I don't want you anywhere near when this goes down."

"I love you," I whispered.

"You shouldn't."

"I know."

The next day, as I traveled on the Union Pacific Rail Road headed to Sacramento, I had time to reflect upon my choices. Brack was more than likely springing himself from jail at that very moment. Earlier, I had broken off my engagement to Edmund. He had taken the news poorly, blaming my hasty decision on the stress of the derailment and my Indian kidnapping.

He had said, "You're not yourself right now, my dear. You'll see things differently when you get home. Your parents will talk some sense into you."

As far as I was concerned, my engagement was over.

Isabelle returned to Chicago. There was no need to accompany me to California now, since there wouldn't be a wedding. I considered her one of my closest friends, whether I married her brother or not. I would write her letters for the rest of my life. Millie, my stalwart companion, forever loyal, no matter how ridiculous my decisions were, was with me on the train.

Hours outside of Sacramento, she tossed a paper on the table. We were in the dining car having tea. "This might interest you."

The headline read: *Corbett Gang. Brazen Jail Break! Brack Corbett, Buck Bass, and Jimmy McCarty escaped the Madison County lockup after obtaining a weapon from an unidentified female. Responsible for the B&O train robbery, the bandits made off with more than twelve thousand dollars in cash and jewelry. These men are considered armed and dangerous.*

Millie sat across from me. "An unidentified female?"

"What a hussy," I whispered, not wanting to be overheard by the people sitting behind us. "Look. May's Department store is having a sale." I pointed to the paper. "Isn't that delightful?"

Millie pursed her lips. "Splendid."

I laughed, feeling ridiculously happy.

That evening, as we disembarked, I saw my parents in the crowded station, my mother pointing in my direction. "There she is!" My mother, a statuesque blonde, was dressed in gray satin; her fitted jacket had a huge bow at the front, and her skirts were gathered and draped with a bustle. "Oh, my darling! What an adventure!" She embraced me, smelling of something floral and exotic. "We were so worried." Her English accent was pronounced.

"I'm fine."

"You were so brave, my dear. How awful to have fallen victim to the Indians."

"They're no worse than the *Azande*."

"Oh, they were indeed fearsome, weren't they? Bones through their noses and filed teeth." She shivered.

I linked my arm through hers. "I have so much to tell. I'm not getting married to Edmund after all."

"What?" My father, whose graying hair was hidden under a hat, was a step before us. "What do you mean?" His accent held a hint of twang.

"I wondered why Isabelle wasn't here," said mother.

"I've set my cap on someone else."

"Oh, darling. Don't tell me that. The invitations have all gone out."

The grin on my face could hardly be contained. "Daddy, you'll love him. He's a bit of a scoundrel, but then again, you're fond of the unusual, aren't you?"

"What's this about?" He'd stopped walking.

"I've fallen in love with a train robber."

My mother gasped.

The next morning, I knocked on the door of my father's study. "Daddy?"

"Come in." Floor to ceiling shelves lined the walls, filled with books and colorful art from Africa. There was an ivory tusk resting on a lacquered wooden stand. "What is it, pumpkin?"

"I need your help with something."

He'd been out with the horses, and he still had on his riding boots. Sitting in a comfortable looking leather chair, he rested his feet on the desk. "Shoot. What is it?"

"I think I might leave. I might live in South America."

"What?"

"I need to book passage to Peru."

"Why the hell would you do that? You just got here. Who do you know in South America?"

"I've made a mess of things. I've...fallen for the wrong man...but I want to make it right."

"I thought you were kidding about that train robber." He sat forward, a look of concern etched into the lines on his forehead. "You can't be serious about this Corbett fellow. You didn't really take up with a bank robber, darlin'. Tell me it's not true."

"He's a train robber...and I love him." I squared my shoulders, as my lips thinned into a grim, yet determined, line.

"Jesus Christ! Your mother's gonna kill you. I should take you over my knee and slap some sense into you. I really should."

A knock sounded on the door. "Miss Collins," said an accented voice. "Your guests are here."

Excitement raced through me. "They are?"

"Yes, Miss." The maid wore a black frock with a white apron.

"Where are they?"

"In the parlor."

"Thank you."

My father glared at me. "What have you done now?"

"Well…" I took a deep breath. "It looks like you might have grand children."

His mouth fell open. "You're carrying that bandit's baby?"

"No. He already has children."

"So?"

"Well, they're here now, and…they're mine." I'd shocked him into uncharacteristic silence. "Say something, daddy."

"Your mother's gonna kill you. You can't seriously be considering this, honey."

"This is what I want," I said simply, knowing that I had made the right decision.

He seemed to consider his words carefully. "You love that man that much?"

Tears welled in my eyes. "Yes, daddy."

Chapter Seventeen

It wasn't a question of what I would do for love. It was a question of what I wouldn't do. That answer was easy. I waited for Brack to arrive, standing on the balcony of the house my parent's had built, the land stretching out as far as the eye could see. It was sunset, and the sky was tinged with bluish orange bands of clouds. The Spanish hacienda was newly built, the smell of fresh paint lingering. A lone horse appeared in the distance, its rider dressed darkly and wearing a wide-brim hat.

Anxious bundles of energy raced through me, and I hastened to the door, flinging it open and rushing down the landing to the staircase. The double doors of the entry were cast open under my direction, the warm breeze of summer touching my skin. Flowers in pots threw splashes of color against the terracotta tiles. The aroma of honeysuckle and wild rose lingered pleasantly. A groom came out to get the horse, the rider dismounting determinedly, glancing in my direction. The fabric of my dressing gown caught the breeze, as I ran towards the object I so desired.

"Brack!" I flung myself at him, and he grabbed me. "Oh, Brack!"

"You're the craziest woman I ever met."

"I'll be the craziest woman you ever married."

"You better think long and hard before committing to a degenerate like me."

Our lips met, igniting an incredible kiss. "Let's talk in my bedroom," I breathed.

"Your parents."

"They're in town. It's just us."

"I didn't go through all this trouble to have somebody's daddy shoot me for messin' with his little girl."

"Brack." Steel laced my voice. "I'm a grown woman. If I want to sleep with a man, I will. What happens in my bedroom is nobody's business."

"Well then...it'd do no good to argue with you. You seem awful determined to get me naked."

"Oh, you've no idea," I giggled, grasping his hand, dragging him towards the house. Once in my room, I untied the laces on the front of my dress. It was like a dream having him here with me. I'd waited for days. "Are you hungry? Thirsty?"

"I had dinner when I got the horse. It's sittin' like a brick in my stomach."

"Oh, no," I laughed. "That's terrible."

He removed his jacket and waistcoat, leaving the items over a chair. Then he stepped out of his boots and began to unbutton his shirt. "I can't stay long. I gotta get my kids. I'm plannin' on running to Mexico."

I lifted the dress over my head, standing naked before him. "We'll talk about that in a minute." I ran my hand across the firm expanse of his chest, feeling the wild staccato of his heart. "Did you miss me?"

"I'd say so." He grabbed me. "I still can't believe a blonde with big tits broke me outta jail." His mouth brushed my neck, teeth nipping at my skin. "Nobody's ever done anything like that for me before."

"I want you, Brack Corbett. I broke off my engagement for you. I broke the law for you. I gave you my heart. I would've given you my virginity, but that horrible Indian got there first."

"None of that matters," he rasped.

"Oh, Brack. Kiss me."

"Yes, ma'am."

A hand cupped my breast, the nipple hardening instantly, producing a rush of desire that left my knees weak. He lifted me into his arms, swinging me towards the bed. He'd shaved, revealing the clean planes of his face, high cheekbones, and a strong jawline.

"What happened to Buck and Jimmy?"

"They split up. It's every man for himself. You sure are gorgeous."

"Thank you, Mr. Corbett. I've missed you."

"I bet you have."

I wrapped a hand around his throbbing cock. "I've missed this too."

"Yeah?" His grin was sinful.

His lips descended to my neck, where he kissed and nibbled his way to my breasts. The silky globes were manipulated in his hands, and my nipples suckled into stiff peaks, wet and chilled by the air. A hand drifted down my belly towards my pussy, which was damp and eager for his touch. A finger dipped into the swollen folds, finding my entrance.

"Oh, Brack…"

He worked a finger in, wiggling it around and drawing it in and out. "You like that?" he sounded hoarse.

"Yes."

He kissed his way to my tummy, his mouth replacing his finger, covering me with heat. A firm tongue pushed against my clit, creating a firestorm of sensation. I sighed, as I stared at the canopy of the bed. Yards of sheer white fabric filled my vision. While he worked my nub, he drove two fingers into my soggy pussy. The sensations this provoked proved to be too much, and my body suddenly tensed, shuddering, finding release.

"Brack!"

"Well, Jesus," he murmured. "That didn't take long."

"Sorry." A knock sounded at the door. "Go away." It swung open, revealing Millie, who wasn't surprised to find Brack in my room. "Millie! I'm reuniting with my handsome. Must you interrupt at this very minute?"

She closed the door behind her. "The little ones are settled."

"You could've waited until later to tell me." My tone betrayed my irritation.

"I thought you might need help."

"With Mr. Brack?" That was a surprise.

"Or with you."

"Oh…Millie…that's naughty."

"What exactly are you proposing?" drawled Brack. "You don't seem too inclined towards the opposite sex. But you like the same sex, don't you?"

"My only concern is the welfare and education of Miss Collins." She moved hair away from my shoulder, her eyes lingering on my breasts. "Her happiness is foremost in my thoughts."

"Honey, if you're gonna barge into my bedroom and fondle my wife, you better be prepared to do us both." His cock had her attention, the tip glistening with clear fluid.

"Oh, Millie." My inhibitions seemed to have disappeared. "We should suck him together. Then we can take turns riding him."

Brack's smile was huge. "I've just died and gone to heaven."

Millie met my stare. "I'll sit on his face. You suck him."

"Oh, my goodness." I was stunned by her suggestion.

"If you wanna smother me with that pussy, then so be it."

Needing no further encouragement, Millie stripped off her blouse and skirt, straddling him, lowering to his mouth. She sighed blissfully, as his tongue entered her. "Oh, yeeesss…"

I grasped his cock, which felt sticky from his own emissions, and suckled the tip, making noisy squashing sounds. Brack murmured something incoherent. Millie began to shift her hips, driving herself over him, wetting his face with the juices of her arousal. I worked the shaft, licking the length of each side all the way to the base. His soft balls were in my hands, pulled away from his body and in my mouth, being sucked and prodded with my tongue. From there I laved my way up to the rounded tip, sucking forcefully, producing a series of manly groans.

"Oh, dear!" gasped Millie. "It's so good. I won't…be able…ooohhhh…" Her chin tipped upward, hair falling over the bed, as she shuddered, her body finding release.

Brack moaned, sounding as if he were in agony. The tip erupted with a jet of silky semen, bursting out in measured pulses, flinging across his belly. I closed my lips around him, tasting the musky confection. Then I set about sucking him clean, lapping up every salty drop.

"Oh, honey…"

Millie collapsed on the bed. "Thank you," she murmured. "I think I'll go now."

Brack's laughter filled the room. "You're a piece of work, woman. I bet I'll never figure you out."

She slid from the bed, snatching her clothing from the floor. "It's all right. I'll never understand myself either." She glanced at me. "Shall I bring them in?"

"Yes. I'll get dressed."

"Bring what in?" He sounded tired.

"A surprise." I threw his shirt at him. "Put something on."

"Yes, ma'am."

I got on the bed and snuggled into him, his arm going around me. "Brack?"

"Yeah?"

"What do you say we take a little trip?"

"I gotta get my kids. Then I say we head south."

"That's exactly what I was thinking. We leave tomorrow."

"Well, that's a bit soon. I gotta get to Missouri first, honey. That'll take days. I'll be lucky if I don't get caught. I was thinkin' of wearing some sort of disguise, maybe shaving my head or something. Them damn Wanted posters are everywhere."

There was a knock on the door. "Come in." I sat up. "All of that won't be necessary."

Millie entered with two children who had been bathed, groomed, and dressed in brand new outfits. Brack, recognizing his own flesh and blood, sprang from the bed.

"Jesus!" His astonished look brought an enormous smile to my face. "JESUS!" He ran fingers through his hair, blinking, yet not believing what he was seeing. "Is this real?"

"They sure were a mess when we got them," said Millie. "Under all that dirt and grime, I found adorable children. One was even a girl."

"Daddy?"

Tears brimmed in Brack's eyes. "Melanie." The little girl bounded over, the doll in her arms falling to the floor. "Daddy!"

He got down on his knees and caught her. Her brother took a tentative step. Brack held out his hand. "Come here, son." That was all the encouragement he needed, and he flung himself at his father. The three of them embraced for long minutes, while I stared at Millie. Both of us blinked back tears.

"You did a good thing, Sarah. It was probably the dumbest thing you've ever done...but it was a good thing."

I sniffed. "Thank you, Millie."

The End

A preview of
Cum For The Viking
by Virginia Wade

Lora's Seduction

Chapter One

"So, who is my husband, mother?"

She stared into a bowl, while the wind howled outside, bringing a northern gale. "He's not from around here."

I'd begged her for years to read the leaves, to see my future, and she had finally capitulated. I sat on the end of a rickety chair, waiting anxiously to hear her precious words. Her readings were always accurate. This was why the women in the village harassed us day and night, begging to know their future. Mother, being far too honest for her own good, had angered many with her less than tactful responses. If she saw death, she said so. If she saw misfortune, she said so. Her predictions had always come to pass, and enemies had been made. The future could not be altered; it was predestined, created by the forces of the universe.

She moved the bowl, rearranging the leaves, her brows drawing together. "I see...an invasion." This declaration seemed to surprise her.

"What?"

"They're coming," she whispered.

"But what about my husband? I'm tired of being alone. I want a man to warm my bed." The men in the village shunned me, as they did my mother, although some of them didn't hesitate to come calling in the middle of the night. *Witches, the women cried when they saw us. Harlots!* I'd had stones thrown at me my entire life. "You said I'd have love. You said I'd be worshiped. I'm tired of waiting, mother."

"You'll be worshipped, my dear. Your husband comes…but he's not what you think he is."

And now she would channel magic and speak in riddles. "Go on." I watched her carefully, her nearly black hair falling over her shoulders.

"He's a great and powerful man—"

"You mustn't humor me! I can handle the truth. I know I'll be a farmer's wife. I'm fully prepared to yoke oxen to the plough."

She held up a hand. "No. That isn't what'll happen, Lora. You're not destined to work the fields. You'll have all the pretty things you want with a pretty house. I see children. Several. But…"

"But what?" I rested my elbows on the table.

"There's some confusion here. I see two men, but only the dark haired one will be your love, your protector. He's foreign."

"He'd have to be," I said bitterly. "No one in the village would marry me."

Her eyes met mine. "We have so little time."

"Will something happen soon?"

"This means change." She pointed to the clumps of moist tealeaves around the edges of the bowl. "Great change comes, but you must be careful. I must be careful." Her gaze took on a faraway look. "I must plan."

"Will you travel again?"

"Yes."

My heart sank. "Why?"

"The future I see isn't mine. I'd only get in the way. I'm going inland. I'll stay with my sister."

I lay my hand on hers. "Don't go. You've only just returned. I hate it when you leave me."

"You won't be alone for long. He comes soon. He's going to take you away." Her eyes watered. "Your future is far away from here."

A part of me hoped she was wrong, and the other part prayed she was right. I'd been an outcast my entire life, and my prospects were bleak. Men went out of their way to avoid me, fearing me and the powers they thought I possessed. I wasn't a witch, but I did know the healing arts and how to derive medicines from plants. My mother was the gifted medium. I didn't possess her skills.

"I wish you'd stay."

"I leave in the morning."

Alarm raced through me. "So soon?"

"Yes, my dear. I'm sorry."

I slept horribly that night, tossing and turning; the straw mattress was lumpy and uncomfortable. The wind howled, the sides of our wattle-and-daub hut shaking. The thatch on the roof would require patching in the morning. My mother was up before me, making the fire and packing her belongings. I gazed at her, feeling a sense of loss.

"Are you sure about this?"

She glanced over her shoulder. "Yes."

"You've been wrong before."

"Lady Abbot tricked me with false questions, Lora. She was playing games. I'm never wrong." She muttered under her breath, "That woman will get hers soon enough."

"I wish you'd stay." I swung my legs over the bed.

"Take what vegetables you can from the garden. Kill the chickens. Eat well, my dear. Food will be scarce."

"Did you have a dream?"

"Men are coming. The sea will be filled with red sails. Go to the woods when this happens. Stay there as long as you can."

Fear lodged in my gut. "How much time do I have?"

"A day, maybe. Perhaps less." She came to the bed, touching my face. "You're the most beautiful girl. You're my salvation. Your father, God rest his soul, would've been proud of the woman you've become. I'm proud to be your mother. I'm sorry for the trouble I've caused, but it is as it should be."

I grabbed her hand. "Don't go."

"I must."

She folded a small crust of bread in a cloth. "Use the rest of the wheat. Fortify yourself."

"I will." I hugged her. "Will I ever see you again?"

She smiled sadly. "No." Her gray gown hung loosely on her thin frame. A brown cloak went over her shoulders, and leather slippers were on her feet. "Heed my words, Lora. They'll come to pass."

"Yes, mother." I followed her out, the wind catching my hair and a biting cold lashing my face. I watched her walk down the path, her figure growing smaller and smaller. "Goodbye," I whispered.

I spent the day gathering vegetables, making bread, and slaughtering the chickens, which I cut up into a stew. I would feast tonight. It was almost a shame to waste all this food on one person. The wind drove the rain against the side of the house, dampening the clay, water leaking in. The smell of moist earth assailed me along with the tantalizing aroma of chicken stew. I ate until my tummy bulged, satiated on the nourishing supper. Then I heated water and prepared a bath, using a cloth to wipe myself clean. I would wash my hair afterwards, dunking my head in the bucket. When this task was complete, I sat before the fire, warming my bones and drying my hair, using a wooden comb to remove the tangles.

A scratching on the door garnered my attention. This was followed by a soft, "Meow."

"Vincent?" I opened the door, a gust of freezing rain wetting my face. "Where have you been?" The black cat rubbed against my leg. I hadn't seen him in two weeks. He looked well fed, which was astonishing. "You naughty cat. What mischief have you gotten into?"

"Purrrr…"

He sat before the fire and began to preen himself, licking his black, lustrous coat. I joined him, scratching behind his ears. "I'm so glad you're back. I won't be alone now."

"Purrr…meow…"

He slept in my bed, curled up next to me, keeping me warm. A noisy seagull woke me the next morning, and I dragged myself from the bed to light the fire. I ate a bowl of soup, filling my belly to capacity. Then I dunked the bread into the mixture and ate that as well. The gale had died down, the rain stopping for the moment. Wrapping a cloak around myself, I left the house to check for damage. I might have to repair the leaks before they worsened. A mist lingered, the fog so thick I could barely see five feet before me. Remembering my mother's words, I wandered towards the cliffs to look down into the harbor, although, with the fog, I doubted I would see anything at all.

The invigorating cold roused my spirits. I loved this walk. On a clear day, the beauty of the ocean stretched out as far as the eye could see, but today the mist had yet to lift. I sat on a rock near the cliff edge and listened. It was eerily quiet. I lingered for more than an hour, the air chilling me thoroughly, and waited. There was a part of me that knew once the fog cleared, I would see my mother's vision. I feared this, yet I understood it was my future. The sun poked through the clouds briefly, enough to burn away the blanket of haze that refused to budge. It was then that I caught a glimpse of red. I sat straight and squinted, trying to get a better look.

I gasped. The opening in the fog revealed ships, lots of ships! Were they merchant vessels coming into port? They looked utterly unfamiliar, which was worrying. Their shapes were long and sleek, with dragon-shaped prows and high curving sterns. Billowing red sails filled my vision. Bells began to ring in the village, the inhabitants having seen the approaching threat, but it was too late.

"God help us," I whispered. These were no merchant vessels. This was an invading force, and they would wreak havoc, no doubt. I sprang to my feet, hastening to the house, where I packed quickly; throwing whatever food items I could find into a sack. "Vincent? Where are you, you silly cat?" I had the clothes on my back and my cloak. I was fortunate enough to have shoes. My mother had traded her psychic services to a tradesman for leather slippers.

Most of the villagers went barefoot.

I left the house, the wooden door slamming behind me. I knew where I would go, but I dreaded it. Hurrying for the forest, the faint sounds of screams reached my ears. I ran down the path, the heavy sack slung over my shoulder and my heart thundering in my chest. I darted into the safety of the trees, finding the refuge I needed. My legs carried me to a small cave my mother had discovered years ago, while seeking protection from the villagers, who wanted to burn her for witchcraft. She had lived in the hideaway for more than a year, only returning when it was safe. That had been Lady Abbot's doing, but I suspected it was more out of jealousy, because of Lord Abbot's attentions towards her. We were hated for a number of reasons. Firstly, my mother's fortune telling abilities, then my particular success with healing herbs, and then our beauty, of course. The Green women were renowned for their lustrous black hair, pale, unblemished skin, impossibly large breasts, and heart-shaped faces, which were bordered by delicately arching brows. I had always known my mother was stunning, and, after father had died, the men came around. Married, single, and engaged, it didn't matter. She attracted them by the droves, and they brought gifts: chickens, wine, cheeses, and silver. I would be made to wait in the cold, while she let them have her body, her moans of pleasure seeping through the clay and wattle walls.

As I grew and my figure filled out, I also received the attention of the village men, who leered at me from their carts and horses, calling me rude names. I'd been attacked once, on the road to Dorset, but I always carried a knife, sheathed on my thigh, and I had stabbed him in the arm, frightening the scoundrel off.

The men avoided me after that, but they would stare, hunger flaring in their eyes.

The cave was hidden behind a rocky outcropping, and I hadn't been here since my mother's banishment. It smelled of damp earth, decaying detritus, and limestone. I found a wooden chest against a wall, which held an old blanket, several candles, and a small cauldron. I spent the day collecting firewood and boiling water, and, after the sun went down, I sat by the fire, staring into the bluish-yellow flames, and listened to the sounds of screams from the village.

Chapter Two

On the fourth day of my isolation, I became desperate, not having eaten anything substantial in more than two days. I scoured the forest searching for berries and mushrooms. I tried to catch fish in a stream. I collected minnows instead and ate them raw, out of sheer need. Exhausted and weak, I wandered further from the cave, hoping to find anything that would fill my belly.

The ground suddenly thundered with the sound of horses. This sent me into the underbrush, crouching and hiding from the strangers who approached, but I foolishly stepped on a branch, the wood snapping loudly under my foot. There was movement in the trees, and I fled in the other direction, the ends of my cloak flying out behind me. In my panic, I stumbled, tumbling over knotted roots and falling hard. I struggled to breathe, the wind having been knocked out of me. A boot appeared to my right, scuffed and worn looking. As I gazed up, I felt the cold end of a sword pressed to my neck.

"What have we here?" said a heavily accented voice.

Terror gripped me, my body trembling. *I will die now or worse.* The emptiness of my stomach was long forgotten, replaced by the knowledge that the person who stood over me was one of the invaders. He was shockingly tall, blonde, and heavily outfitted with a helmet, shield, and chainmail. The sword was still pressed to my neck, cold and unyielding. The man with him spoke in a language I didn't understand, and the blonde smiled, his face transforming into a handsome visage. He removed his sword.

"Get up." I struggled to my feet, and he grabbed me, dragging me to him. Interest flared in his pale blue eyes. "It's a dark angel." I pushed against the solid mass of his chest, and he laughed, "You're no match for me, little one. What's your name?"

"Lora." My hand drove into my cloak, to my thigh, where I snatched my knife. "Who are you?"

"Bram Laxdale."

"You Viking scum!" I spat.

He threw his head back in laughter, his Adam's apple moving beneath the skin. I took that moment to press the knife to his arrogant throat. His eyes widened with surprise. His friend spoke then, and the blonde answered, his expression was considering. My knife was sharp, and it punctured the pale skin, producing a single drop of blood. He swiped my arm aside, sending the weapon flying. Strong fingers gripped my hair, pulling me nearer. I was so close I could smell his breath, which was laced with the honeyed aroma of mead.

"This one is mine. She'll tickle my cock nicely."

His friend spoke, the language of Old Norse sounding alien and vulgar. I had been expecting to be raped or worse. I would be lucky to survive the night, but the closeness to this pale stranger had an unusual effect on me. I could feel the vibrancy of his energy, heady and raw. He would be all muscle beneath the encumbrances of war, and this oddly excited me. I'd resented my virginity, wishing it were gone for years now, craving the touch of a man, but none of the villagers would have me. They feared me as a witch, and they cursed and spat whenever I set foot in town. The Green women had always been reviled and spurned.

"*Friðr*," he breathed, desire flaring in his eyes.

He spoke to his friend, his grip tightening. Then he

dragged me with him, his strength beyond comprehension. A horse waited in the thicket, the animal having been tethered to a branch. I was lifted onto it, the Viking settling behind, his steely arm around my tummy. He called out, and the animal bounded forward, the hooves tossing up clumps of earth. The cold wind of autumn sent my hair flying. We emerged from the forest to gallop across farmland, the greenness of the fields stretching on for miles. Plumes of smoke dotted the landscape; fires burned, undoubtedly set by the marauders. Corpses were left to rot on the side of the road; most were bodies of young men and farmers, who had fought bravely with pitchforks and shovels, which were no match for battle-axes and swords.

The harbor had become a fortified Viking camp, outfitted with newly erected walls and a formidable looking gate. The streets teemed with the fair-haired scoundrels, who wore iron helmets and chainmail. The dragon ships dotted the sea, their red sails having been furled. It was an ominous scene, filled with the smell of decomposition and the smoke from a hundred fires.

"She's a witch!" screamed an old woman, who sat in the muck on the side of the road. I glanced at the hag, recognizing her. "Your Viking cock will rot off, if you fuck her." She laughed, the sound grating.

I glanced at Bram Laxdale, his pale eyes glinting with amusement. "Did you hear that, you dumb oaf? I'm a witch. I'm bad luck. Release me before it's too late." Something struck me then, a rock thrown by a villager, no doubt. I held the side of my face, my cheek smarting. Several elderly women loitered, their faces caked with grime. Our horse trotted on, snorting his displeasure at the hostile crowd.

"Witch!"

"Evil Green woman!"

…"fuck her at your own risk, Viking filth!" This was followed by more laughter and insults.

It was disheartening to know that I might be safer with an invading army than my own people. We dismounted on the beach; an assemblage of tents stretched out as far as the eye could see. The structures were covered in a roughly woven material, hopefully watertight, to keep the rain at bay and protect the inhabitants from the elements. A strong hand gripped my arm, dragging me along, the sounds of chaos echoing in my ears, punctuated by screams. Bram seemed to be in a position of power among his men, because they nodded deferentially towards him, as we passed. He tossed open the flap of the tent and shoved me inside. It was dark, the sun having set behind the clouds, and there was no light. I sat on something soft, feeling the pelt of a dead animal beneath me.

"Wait here."

He returned a moment later carrying a stack of wood, which he dropped into a sunken pit in the middle of the space. Something sparked then, and the wood ignited, burning brightly. The Viking removed his helmet, revealing thick blonde hair. This was followed by his shield and chainmail. He wore a tunic and shirt with loose fitting braes. I eyed him warily, wondering when he would force himself on me. He poured fluid into a wooden cup and downed the contents in one gulp. Repeating the procedure, he approached me.

"Drink." I took the offering and quaffed it without hesitation, the delicious mead sliding down my throat and warming my empty belly. "Good?" I nodded. His smile was disarming. "You're hungry. Wait here. If you leave, my men will show you no mercy." He stalked from the tent.

I sat and listened to the sounds of arguing and laughing nearby. Swords clashed, followed by shouts of victory. The invaders were relieving boredom and tension by engaging in boisterous play. Bram returned, carrying a large ceramic bowl. My mouth watered instantly, my tummy rumbling at the smell of meat. There were two succulent looking lamb shanks resting on a bed of cabbage. He knelt before me, placing the food at my feet, and, as I grabbed a shank, he removed my cloak, exposing a simple gray dress, hidden behind a woolen tunic.

I ate ravenously, the food utterly delicious, while the Viking worked to remove my clothing, lifting the tunic off and discarding it on a blanket. My shoes and woolly socks were next, followed by my dress, which revealed the first of two long gowns, with tight fitting sleeves. He grasped an arm, trying to remove a gown, while I struggled to eat, tearing away at the meat, which came off the bone easily. My interest in food far outweighed the fact that a stranger was divesting me of my clothing, one piece at a time. I wasn't going to make it easy for him, and I continued to eat, while he struggled to get the second gown off, his face tightening with irritation.

"Put that down for a moment!" His braes bulged in the crotch area. I continued to eat, tearing off another chunk and chewing determinedly. He lifted me to my knees. "When was the last time you've eaten?"

"Two days ago."

He sighed. "Raise your arms." I did so, refusing to let go of the lamb. He pulled the garment over my head, exposing me entirely to his lustful gaze. My breasts, no longer hidden beneath countless layers of clothing, appeared gloriously full and firm. I had never shown them to anyone other than my mother, and, judging from the Viking's reaction, he seemed surprised and slightly stunned by their appearance. "Praise the Gods," he murmured. "You've been blessed by Freya herself."

I had no idea what he was talking about. My focus was on eating, and my teeth ripped off a delicious strip of meat. I eyed the Viking, as he began to remove his shirt and trousers, exposing heavily tattooed arms and a muscled chest, coated in a smattering of nearly white hair. Never having seen a man naked before, this was a forbidden treat, and I stared as his pants lowered, revealing a stiff looking cock. The object between his legs had my undivided attention. I'd even stopped chewing for the moment, to ogle the strange looking protrusion, which rested upon curly blonde hair.

"Never seen one before, have you?" I shook my head, meeting his gaze. "You're going to get to know this one very well."

I swallowed the food in my mouth, ripping off another piece of meat. All that was left now was bone. I grasped a handful of cabbage and brought it to my mouth, chewing indelicately. My dedication to the meal seemed to amuse the Viking. He poured mead and handed me a cup, which I took gratefully and downed within a second.

"Good Lord, woman! You were ravenous."

I belched loudly, surprising myself, yet not caring in the least. He threw back his head and roared with laughter. There was food all over my face. My lack of manners and decorum were a non-issue, because I could have cared less. This might be my last meal on earth, and I was determined to enjoy it. He poured water into a small wooden bowl and dunked a cloth, ringing it out. His thighs touched mine; his legs were three times as big, if not more. I wiped my face and hands clean, lethargy beginning to seep into my bones, producing a lengthy yawn. I'd spent days in the cave not being able to sleep on the cold stone floor. The pelt felt wonderfully soft, cushioned by sand beneath. The warmth of the mead spread through my body, leaving me satiated and content. My immediate needs had been met, and, as I lay on the pelt, I grasped a blanket, bringing it to me. Turning on my side, I closed my eyes.

I felt the Viking's hands on me, touching my arm. If he wanted to rape me, I would not be able to stop him. He had given me shelter, food, and drink. Now all I wanted was sleep. His fingers touched my face gently. Then he murmured something in a language I didn't understand. He shifted, drawing me into his arms, the warmth of his body pressed against me. He smelled of horse and leather, a musky combination that sent pleasurable tingles down my spine. As I drifted into the void of unconsciousness, all I could think of was that I liked this man.

Chapter Three

The squawking of seagulls brought me out of a sound sleep, the chill of morning forcing me to burrow into something warm. A strange hardness pressed against my tummy, wetting me. It was marvelous to wake not feeling exhausted or starving. I remembered the Viking who had found me in the woods, and I knew that I would know him intimately. If the feel of his cock was any indication, he had been awake and waiting for me to stir.

Soft lips touched my neck, sending delicious shivers down my spine, and a muscled arm drew me in. The low and seductive sound of a manly growl filled the tent, a harbinger of sinful things to come. I found myself on my back, the stranger's kisses landing on my neck, sucking and gently biting my flesh. I threaded my fingers through his long, thick hair, enjoying the luxurious sensation. If this was what being raped and brutalized felt like, he could do it to me often. He kissed me then, his tongue entering my mouth. His lengthy form was over me, his cock pressing into my wetness, while he kissed me nearly senseless. I should have been ashamed to find pleasure with a heathen, but my response was a direct result of his skill at seduction.

"Ooohh…" I moaned helplessly, as his hand pressed into my tummy, massaging its way lower. I had lost control, my hips bucking upwards, trying to rub against him. My fingers gripped the muscles in his shoulders. "Oh, no…"

"Yes," he murmured.

Pleasurable tingles erupted, which centered in my belly and fanned out to every part of my body. He stroked my nub, wetting himself in my arousal. I tossed my head back, overwhelmed, because the sensations were rapturous and sinful. His fingers drove between the swollen lips, spearing me with their thickness. A sudden, inexplicable burst of pain registered, and I gasped.

"Ouch!"

He froze, his face in my neck, his breathing labored. "You're virgin."

"Yes." He moved within me slowly, but it hurt, so I clamped my legs together, trying to force him out. "Ouch." He exhaled his frustration and closed his mouth around a nipple, which he suckled. I tried to dislodge his hand, but he insisted on driving in further, adding to the sensation of pain. "Oh, stop!" His thumb moved over my clit, rubbing me to pleasure, yet again, but the intrusion continued to sting with discomfort. "Please stop."

He withdrew and sucked his finger into his mouth. "I taste blood."

I didn't want to look at him out of embarrassment. I could feel the skin on my chest flushing. He grasped my breasts, pressing them together and laving them one at a time. His attention turned towards my tummy and lower, where his mouth lingered over me. It was mortifying, because he was so close to an unmentionable place.

"Oh, no, you mustn't." But it was too late, as he licked my clit, leaving a path of wetness. The feelings this provoked had me biting my lip to keep from moaning. He slid over my silken nub, wetting me with saliva, while pleasuring me intimately. My fingers threaded through his hair. "Ooohh…" This assault continued for long, spellbinding minutes, the attention relaxing me thoroughly, leaving me trembling and weak. His tongue plunged, spearing and wiggling deeply. Whatever discomfort I had felt was gone, and now only delicious sensations lingered. I tingled everywhere, my stomach shuddering with mini convulsions. The release was building, gathering up the energy to overwhelm me completely. "Oh, Bram!" His mouth pushed me over the edge. I thrust my hips up, wetting his face, while shuddering helplessly. "Ooohhh…Viking!" I collapsed on the pelt, my heart pounding in my chest, as waves of bliss crashed and receded. He kissed me, pillaging my mouth. I could smell myself on him, and it was oddly arousing. His cock pressed against me, urgent and demanding. I wrapped my hand around the throbbing object, feeling wetness.

"Put it in your mouth," he groaned.

That thought was alarming, but a part of me wanted to know what it tasted like. His tongue had been inside of me, after all, intimate and probing. He fell onto his back, his phallus thrusting into the air. My thumb moved over the rounded tip, rubbing away a bead of moisture, but only more appeared. I flung hair over my shoulder, scooting closer, eyeing the lengthy object with interest. The sounds outside the tent revealed a camp coming alive: sporadic male shouts; iron clashing and horses neighing, but none of it mattered because I was about to have my first real taste of the opposite sex. I licked him, surprised by how salty he was.

"That's it…" He smelled musky, yet sweet, his aroma teasing me, compelling me to take even more in my mouth. His fingers drove through the strands of my hair, holding me in place. "More. Eat me, Lora."

He groaned, as I closed my lips around him. It was a thrill, affecting another person in this manner; he was

142

in complete and rapturous pleasure. Now I knew what my mother had done with the men from the village when they had come to call in the middle of the night. I understood why she had enjoyed it so much. Being this close to another person, naked and aroused, was infinitely more satisfying than self-pleasure. We had been taught to fear the raiders from the North, who were rumored to be not only brutal thieves, but cannibals as well. This Viking had shown me nothing but mercy and kindness, and, to thank him, I sucked him whole, swallowing his juices.

"Ooohhh…"

He pressed me to him, the length prodding the back of my throat, choking me. I gagged repeatedly, but this pleased him, because his groans filled the tent. Things seemed to be escalating, the pressure he applied on my scalp increasing. His tummy rippled with hidden muscles, his thighs shaking ever so slightly. Over and over I sucked and gagged, trying to take as much of him as I could.

"*Já*, Lora! Aaachh…"

A burst of warm liquid suddenly erupted in my mouth, and I pulled away, as it shot into the air. Several creamy streams jetted, landing on his belly. He'd closed his eyes; his blonde lashes falling over his cheeks. A pungent, salty taste lingered on my tongue. I snuggled next to him, and he put his arm around me. We'd hardly had the time to recover, when someone appeared at the opening of the tent. The sound of Old Norse shattered the silence.

Bram squeezed me. "I've work to do, my English angel." He stood, naked and proud, the expanse of his muscled chest impressively chiseled. I watched him bathe quickly with a cloth dipped in water. "You mustn't leave this tent." He stared at me. "Do you understand?" I nodded. "I'll have food sent to you." His shirt went over his head, and then he stepped into his braes, pulling them up and hiding his cock. He truly was a magnificent specimen, interlaced with muscles, his shoulders bulging. It was a shame to hide a body like that behind a cloak, which he tied around his neck. He wasn't dressed for battle today, but he did carry a formidable looking sword. He glanced at me briefly and stepped from the tent, leaving me alone in an enemy camp.

Food arrived within minutes, and I ate heartily, delicious chunks of meat in a tasty sauce. I washed with the same cloth Bram had used and made myself presentable. Then I spent the day tidying up the tent, sleeping, and working to untangle my hair. By the time he returned, the sun had set, and a cacophony of noises registered. Men had returned from a day of pillaging.

"So you didn't run after all?" He smiled, his cheeks ruddy from the cold.

"No."

"You're wearing too many clothes."

"I can't be naked all day. It's freezing."

Food arrived, brought in by a boy. He was fair-haired and curious, eyeing me with interest. "Leave it now, Gretter." The boy hadn't understood what he said, so Bram repeated himself in Old Norse. The youngster inclined his head respectfully and darted from the tent. "Come sit; eat."

I scooted next to the Viking, helping myself to a portion of fish. There was a type of bread, which was delicious, and boiled carrots. I glanced at Bram, curious about why his people had invaded us. "How long will you be here?"

"Long enough to finish the job."

"What job?"

"We seek gold and silver and jewels."

"Where do you find those?"

"Mostly in the monasteries and churches."

My heart sank. "You've looted the churches?" He grinned, confirming my thoughts. "But...that's sacrilegious."

He shrugged. "What use has a man of God with such material encumbrances? Shouldn't he be praying for our sins instead of hoarding gold?"

"They do pray for us. They help us."

"How?"

"They...they help the poor. They care for the sick. They offer sanctuary to refugees and serfs." He seemed unimpressed with my examples.

"They only help themselves. Have you any idea how much gold we found today?" He grinned. "I'm rich. I'll be able to pay my debts."

"Excellent. Then I've come at the right time," said a deep, melodic voice. I gasped at the intrusion; a man dressed entirely in black had entered our tent. His cloak was made of mink, and it was soft and warm looking. "How are you, Bram?" His gaze rested upon me. "Ah, the comforts of home. A beautiful woman to warm your bed. It would've surprised me, if you'd been alone."

The Viking's expression changed dramatically, displeasure marring his features. "Matheus Hrolf." The tone in his voice was flat. "What an unexpected surprise. What brings you here?" He muttered, "How did you find me?"

"I've known for some time about this raid. It was no secret."

145

The stranger sat on a pelt, crossing his long legs before him. His looks were as dark as Bram's were pale; brown eyes, thick, russet hair, and the hints of a beard graced his handsome face. His nails were clean, gold and gems flashing from several rings on his fingers. He wore a heavy gold necklace, with a large ruby pendant. There was something about his look that sent tingles into my tummy. He was clearly a man of great wealth, but I didn't sense cruelty in him, only his interest. I had his undivided attention.

"She's lovely."

Bram glanced at me. "She is, isn't she? I found her hiding in the forest."

"And now she warms your bed."

"Indeed she does, but that's not why you came here."

"I'd be remiss not to monitor my investments."

"No. You've come for payment."

He smiled, flashing impossibly white teeth. "That too."

"The raid has only just begun."

Matheus waved a hand. "Don't trouble yourself. This is a gentle reminder of your obligations."

"How could I forget them?" griped Bram. "I feel the noose around my neck every day, you Danish bastard."

"You mustn't be sore. You gambled with my money and lost. Someone always pays the price." His dark gaze lingered on me, and I shivered, my tummy turning over in silken knots.

Bram noticed his interest. "I've a business proposition for you, if you're interested."

"I've never shied away from a venture."

The Viking's eyes were on me, and I got the distinct

impression that I was going to be a part of his "business proposition". "This lovely English lass is Lora. She's shunned by the villagers. They think she's a witch. How much would a virgin be worth?"

"A virgin?" he laughed. "She's been in your company. I doubt she's pure."

"She is."

The stranger appraised me. "She's pretty to be sure, but your debts far outweigh a lovely girl."

"Consider it a down payment."

"You must think me a fool. I could leave this tent and find a woman in five minutes."

"Not one this beautiful. Take your dress off, Lora. Show him what you're hiding."

I bristled, feeling violated and disgusted and used like chattel. I wasn't this Viking's property. "I will not."

Bram's brows lifted. "I beg your pardon?"

I drew away from him, my hand closing on a knife. "I'm not your property."

Matheus Hrolf's expression revealed his amusement, dark eyes flashing. "I'd say you've lost your touch with women, Bram. This one isn't as docile as you thought."

He scowled, looking displeased. "Take the damn dress off!" I was seeing an entirely new and unpleasant side to my gentle lover, who had been sweet and patient with me. Now that I could be used as a commodity, his attitude had changed dramatically. This left a bitter taste in my mouth. He lunged forward. "Must I rip the clothing from your back, woman?" I took that opportunity to strike him with the knife, catching his hand, which bled instantly. "You little bitch!" His fingers wrapped around my wrist, shaking the knife free. He dragged me to him, growling his displeasure. "I should teach you a lesson, you won't soon forget."

I struggled, squirming, trying to free myself from his steely grasp. "No! Viking scum!"

"You seemed to enjoy me enough this morning!" The sound of material ripping was alarming, my tunic shredding in his hands. This was followed by my dress, which he hadn't damaged as badly. I had underthings on, two layers of gowns, which were the only barrier to being exposed entirely.

"I think I've seen enough," murmured Matheus. "You may leave us. I'll take it from here."

"How much is she worth?"

The dark stranger stared at me. "A great deal."

"Fifty percent?"

"Not that much," he laughed. "Perhaps thirty."

"Forty-five."

"Forty, and that's all."

Bram smiled. "Excellent." His azure gaze rested on me. "You're more helpful than I thought. Be sure to please him, Lora. You won't be a virgin when I return."

Read the rest of the adventure in

Cum For The Viking

About the Author

Virginia Wade is the bestselling author of erotica and erotic romance. Known for her Monster Sex series, the *Cum For Bigfoot* saga, she has penned tales in a variety of subjects, such as a modern, naughty retelling of Jane Austen's most popular novels and a series on lusty Vikings, in *Cum For The Viking*, parts 1-6. She has explored sex in outer space with *Bred by the Alien* and taken readers on a journey to ancient Rome in *Conquest of the Gladiator*.

A mother of two, and a wife, she realized a lifelong dream of writing and publishing after her oldest child graduated from high school. Earlier forays into self-publishing yielded few sales, but the experience and knowledge gained were immeasurable. Once she dipped her toes in erotica, with the publication of *Seducing Jennifer*, which has now been retitled, *Jennifer's Anal Seduction*, the possibility of success presented itself, as the story found a home in the Erotica Top 100. Her second story, *Stacy and the Boys*, also rocketed up the charts, reinforcing the idea that writing in this genre was not only fun, but also profitable.

An idea to write a campy, teen horror-fest, with a Sasquatch protagonist, led to the creation of *Cum For Bigfoot*, which is essentially a series of stories spanning several years in the lives of a tribe of Bigfoots and their human lovers. The silliness, the romance, and the sex struck a chord with readers, who enjoyed the adventures of Porsche, Shelly, and Leslie, while the kidnapped teens came to love their hairy abductors. The series is now on its fourteenth installment, with more to follow.

Cum For Bigfoot was featured in the October 2012

issue of *Penthouse Magazine*. The article, "Paranormal Porn", was written by Nick Redfern.

5856722R00092

Printed in Great Britain
by Amazon.co.uk, Ltd.,
Marston Gate.